ALTERED

HELIX

Altered Helix

Stephanie Hansen

*For my kids, Ethan and Jenna.
Without the light and strength you
bring me I could not have accomplished
this.*

PROPHASE

Some dangers come barreling at you like a freight train. Others slide right under your nose without being noticed. When I took the job at the haunted house, I never imagined I'd be kidnapped.

As I'm blacking out, it's my sense of gratitude that brings me peace in my final moments. At least I was able to experience most of my life's desires before the end.

I'd found the siblings for which I'd yearned while growing up. I'd met someone with whom to share the rest of my life. And perhaps best of all, after many years, I was finally able to see my father again.

Ironic, isn't it? To find everything I'd ever desired, just before I die. The black spots in my vision grow closer and closer together until they completely consume my sight. I imagine the cut they'll make in my body when it's gutted. My breathing becomes shallow. Then, I feel the sharp pressure from the point of the blade against my flesh as it breaks through my skin. My body won't move. I want to cry out, but my voice fails me.

PERCEPTION

As I walk through the hallway to the living room, it's disturbingly silent. I don't hear my mother's fingers brilliantly strumming piano keys. The "Silver Clouds Chasing the Moon" by Lang Lang music sheets are strewn chaotically about the room. I close my eyes and focus on my mother's energy. A vision of her on the bench in the garden under the pergola comes to mind.

I leap the stepping-stones, skipping every other. Blue hydrangeas and orange daffodils blur by me. As I approach, I notice the yellow roses are in full blossom, their smell fresh as the tide rolling in. My mother's holding a picture in her hands.

When she looks up, I see tear streaks on her cheeks. I sit down and put an arm around her. She's holding the last photo we took as a family. My eyes zero in on a male, mirror image of myself, my father. I was fourteen then; now I'm seventeen and graduated early. I wish he could've been there to see it. Mother should be holding a photo of my graduation day with all of us in it, smiling.

I squeeze her shoulder as my throat constricts in pain. Without looking up, I can feel my mother's eyes turn to me. I close my eyes and place my wrists on my knees. I begin playing the piece thrown from the stand in our living room by heart, moving my fingers to the rhythm and placing them where the notes should be. She squeezes my shoulder in return.

Walking to the house, she stops and points at the tire swing, offering an aching smile. I hold her hand as the visualization takes me. My father's pushing me at the age of four, and I feel like I'm on one of the roller coasters we drive by on Route 435.

One of the old ones with only a handlebar for safety, no seatbelts. At the top, my stomach floats up, and the view down becomes daunting. The velocity forces me to squeal. I can still picture his smile seeing me enjoy the ride. In the excitement, I let go to raise my hands in glee. I still remember the way his face turned from elation to horror. He moved faster than I could imagine and caught me before I met my imminent doom.

Falling and your father catching you—this is every child's dream.

I awake from the vision to see my mother walking in front of me. She should have an umbrella draped over her shoulder. She belongs in a painting, that's how beautiful she is. Her clothes move with the curves on her body no matter what she wears: dress, jeans, or sweatpants. I skip the stones again so I can arrive in time to hold the door open for her. The silver, ornate door latch curves to my hand. When she walks in, I look at the neighboring houses. They're two stories high and dwarf our ranch house, but I wouldn't have it any other way. I step onto the Tuscan tile surrounded by red and tan marble walls. I almost hit my head on a hanging cooking pot when I turn on our kitchen flat screen. My mother sits at the table and picks up a pencil; I realize what's missing.

Walking to the front door, I assemble the discombobulated music sheets and place them on the stand. My finger trails on the wooden case, and a memory of my father sitting on the couch materializes. I smile, but it quickly fades. He's not really here and every time I try to use perception to find his location, which I assume is Heaven, I see a beach. Peaceful, relaxing, hot enough to bake skin to a crisp, but that can't be where he is, and I can't seem to pick up any more clues. I take a step forward, interrupting my daydream, grip the brassy steel of our doorknob, and pull the door open. I see our paper resting haphazardly against the oak tree. I grab it, remove the wrapper, and turn to the crossword I know my mother's waiting to tackle.

I enter the kitchen and hand my mother the puzzle. She blooms a smile. I sit next to her, peer at the clues, and I point to fourteen across: The Choral. As she turns to me and nods, I know she will write Number Nine before she moves the pencil. It's the perfect question for a pianist like her to answer, Beethoven.

As she finishes and walks to our mountainous recycle pile, she picks up the document on top. The neon green flier for the haunted house flaps as she brings it back to the table. My mother hands me the advertisement. I see the resignation in her face. She's feeling more than just upset with my choice of occupation. As I hone in on her emotions, a box in the attic pops into my head.

When she leaves to shower, I walk to the main hallway and grab hold of the hanging string. I pull on it, and hinges moan as the attic door swings open. The stairs fall almost too quickly to catch, but I reflexively grab the lower rung. Climbing to the attic feels like entering the mouth of a cave—obscure objects loom out of the thick gray around me. I pull another string and the area erupts in light. Boxes, a chest, and a stand-up mirror are in front of me. I know the box I'm looking for is behind the mirror. As I remove the top box the label on the next reflects the name I'd seen in the vision. BRENNAN'S THINGS.

I open the box of my father's belongings like a child opening a gift. A pair of old sneakers is on top with some team jersey below. Underneath that I find a leather-bound folder with papers inside. There are drawings worth showcasing—complex, detailed, and beautiful depictions of everyday life. When I approach a group called BOURGMONT BUILDING, I feel triumphant because this is the haunted house building, until I flip to the drawings. For some reason, the picture my mother had been holding jumps into my mind before I turn the page. Stairs bathed in shadow seem to breathe, empty hallways feel claustrophobic, and chandeliers sway in an unseen breeze. When the water from the shower downstairs stops, I drop the folder and its contents back into the box. I quickly return everything to its place, pull the light switch, and descend the stairs. Mother walks down the hallway just as I'm closing the attic door.

"Austria, what were you doing up there, darling?" she asks me as she dries her long, dark hair with a towel. I remember them telling me about the debate over my name. My mother's piano is an Austria. My father loved sports and knew the Olympics would take place in Austria during my lifetime. It was a meeting of the minds. It seemed the perfect combination to reflect their love for one another, which formed me.

"Oh, just thought I might find something I could use for the haunted house," I say as I follow her to the kitchen. I should've grabbed something up there to support this statement, but she hasn't seemed to catch on to the missing item. The mere mention of my job appears to jumble her. Still I clasp my hands together so they don't feel empty.

"Ah, that would be exciting, to provide something for the haunting. Austria, I know you like the thought of this job, but are you sure you don't want to go to college?" my mother asks me while she chews on her lower lip, a telltale sign that she's never picked up on. My mother shouldn't play poker.

I grab an orange from the fruit bowl at the center of the table and dig into the skin with my fingernail; the citrus smell over-powering the tension in the room. Lately, it seems like we're constantly at battle. She's forever handing me college brochures that I try to ignore. She's always mentioning how much college can help my career. College is also an expectation from my private schooling. I'm just not ready. I don't know what I want to be for the rest of my life yet.

I take a bite of my orange, and the tang's almost too much for my empty stomach to handle.

Since I moved in with Tiff a couple months ago, my mother's chances of talking me into college have dwindled. I still come to the house every Saturday night, stay over, and spend Sunday with her. It's the only ritual we've remained loyal to since my moving out. It's what my father would've insisted upon, had he not died. The house has become awkward without him. Even though she tries to hide it from me, my mother's been heartbroken. Since I graduated early and moved in with Tiff, she's been able to become a travelling pianist, which had been her dream until she became pregnant with me at the age nineteen, and she and my father married. He would've supported her living her dream, but she couldn't fathom being away from me. She still can't; that's why I had to leave, so she could finally be set free. The door to her soundproof music room finally opens, melodic meditation floating in the air.

An announcement on the television interrupts my train of thought, "Adam Sheffield has done it again. He's reclaimed another old building, one by one turning economically depressed areas into trendy, upbeat attractions. If he keeps this up, he'll do to Kansas City what he's done before in many other cities." As the reporter talks, I think of all the history this Adam guy's removing from our city and all of the ways he finds to do it. Since the dissolution of our national government, there have been many changes. States have tried to take over, and Adam Sheffield is one of their key players. My mother's staring at me when the report stops.

"Hello, Earth to Austria, we were discussing the possibility of college. I'm just trying to look out for you."

"We've discussed this. I just don't know what I want to do in life. Do you want me to spend money on the wrong education?"

She begins nervously tearing the corner off of the poster. "I understand, but why the haunted house? I know Tiff works there, but don't other things interest you?"

"I feel like at the haunted house I'm able to step outside of my comfort zone and see what's out there. Maybe I can even write a script for one of the scenes. Why do you not like the idea of me working there so much?"

"You don't know what has taken place in that building. When your father and I lived there, he experienced more than strong perceptions, almost telepathy in its truest form, but he couldn't figure out what was speaking to him."

Just then, there's a honk outside. Tiff and Bill are picking me up today so we can move some things we need out of storage to the building. I give my mother a kiss on the cheek.

"Everything's going to be fine," I attempt to assure her.

She hugs me tightly before I leave.

PREMONITIONS

Not only is the oxygen nearly depleted from my lungs after moving and unloading numerous boxes today, but the thick heat in Bill's car is suffocating me. I wonder if maybe he could acquire an air conditioning unit that works for his car as I force my arm to roll down the window. As the fresh air hits me, relief washes over me, but I can still feel the redness in my face, sweat dampening my hairline. Bill's hearse is an ancient car made of heavy metal instead of the light aluminum, plastic, and fiberglass used in modern vehicles. I refer to these types of old vehicles as tanks. The front seat, just like the back seat, is all one piece once the armrests are raised. What makes Bill's hearse unique is the paintings of walking zombies and blood-dripping vampires on the side panels.

Tiff nudges me with her elbow. "Still glad you succumbed to my insistence that you sign up for this, Austria?" She raises an eyebrow as she asks, referring to our afternoon of hard labor.

Tiff has a warm smile, and her face is surrounded by curly blonde locks. Many people get along with her. Right now, I'm not sure I'm one of them.

"Tiff, you know this is better than going to college fumbling over what major to choose."

We both smile. She knows I'll take physical work over having to figure out what to do with my life. She's been at my house when my mother and I have practiced Chopin, perfection expected. She gives me a sideways glance. All of a sudden, my mind sees the haunted house suffering a horrible demise. Maybe my seeing is off, and I've allowed my mother's warnings to influence me. Mother seems so against me working in this particular building because of something that occurred when she and Father were here, like there's a lurking spirit. I think that's just one more reason I'm intrigued by the job; it's a way to connect with him on some level. It's not like I can take the bus to Heaven and visit him. Maybe, she just doesn't understand how much I miss him, but that can't be it either.

Bill chimes in from the driver's seat. "Give it a chance to grow on you."

My mind picks up on his thoughts: there are many people out there without jobs at all, but the haunted house industry's currently pulsing with excitement. In the past, paranormal buzz brought people to haunted houses, but with the decline of the economy at the government's fall, more and more dollars are spent on affordable entertainment. Bill knows a lot about those without jobs. He houses half the street kids in this city when they no longer can find a couch to crash on, because he's been there himself. With the end of national government assistance, states have fumbled trying to care for those in need.

"Hey Bill, can I have a chance to mock up the scenes?" I ask as I try to focus on the job despite nagging worries about my mother and people without homes.

There's a pause, and when I look at Bill to see if he's going to answer, I'm disheartened. Images of carnage fill my mind. I don't know where they come from, but it's like flashbacks of a war scene aftermath. Bill isn't responding. Even after Tiff tugs his sleeve, he doesn't look at us or say a word.

Tiff and I turn our heads away from Bill to see what he's looking at. As he parks in front, we see what grabbed his attention. Every single prop and costume that we'd taken in is now strewn about outside. A zombie costume has landed on a bush, bent backward in an unnatural pose. Its position is almost poetic, like a Poisson ballerina move. The wig on the ground a few feet away looks as though it could be rising from the grave. What's worse is that every window of the house is shattered. It looks as if something blew up inside, forcing everything out. As I focus on the building, I see there isn't more damage inside. Could this have anything to do with what my mother warned me about? At least the bones of the structure seem to be intact—shattered windows and props scattered about appear to be the extent of the damage.

Bill steps out of the car and is pacing back and forth. He's pale, as though he's seen a ghost. He looks at the building as if it's his child. I can understand why Bill loves this building. There are gargoyles on the rooftop ledges. The craftsmanship in the statues and every laid brick is something that hasn't existed for years. At the two front corners of the roof there are lion gargoyles, poised in a pouncing stance. It feels as though any moment they could come to life and you'd become their prey— the perfect ambiance for a haunted house.

Tiff and I exit the car to join Bill and walk around picking up some of the things that blew out of the building. Luckily, most seem to be undamaged. I try to focus on the energy of these things, but there's a wall blocking my perception. I can't see what caused this. Bill, who has been on the phone the past couple minutes, returns the phone to his pocket.

"Window repairs can be made this afternoon. Let's assess the status inside before we do anything with the props out here." Bill now has his hands in his pockets and is rocking from heel to toe. He seems to be in shock and no wonder, such drastic harm to your life's work can't be easy to take. There's no reason for any of this. Why would someone target something as innocent as a haunted house?

"How in the world did this happen?" Tiff asks as she puts a comforting hand on Bill's shoulder.

I'm asking myself the same question, prodded by the cloud obscuring my vision.

We were only gone fifteen or twenty minutes. How could something that took us hours to do unravel in such a short time? I wonder how Bill's going to afford window repairs and why my ability isn't picking up on what happened here. It's like when my father was taken away from me, a complete mystery.

"I have no clue how this happened. It almost looks as if it combusted internally," Bill says, rubbing the back of his neck. Then he grabs a tool case from the car and heads inside. At least I know he will find the interior mostly intact, as that was one of the insights given to me before my ability failed. I see a look of despair and anger as Bill takes in the scene in front of us. He has to believe the inside is damaged, given the evidence out here.

We walk to the building. The doors are fifteen feet tall, decorative and sturdy enough to last a century or more if not two. As we enter, the building smells like an old book when you open it and put your nose to the pages. The hallways are dark even though it's midday, but I'm able to pick up most of the details. I'm amused by the sight of genuine cobwebs that will be cleaned away so that we can set up fake ones. How did they survive the blast that threw everything outside? The air's hot and musty, but so far everything inside seems to be as it had been. There isn't any damage to the walls or the floors. It's as though whatever caused this only affected the costumes, props, and windows. Does it not want us here?

We head back to the inventory room where we'd set up all of the props and costumes. On the way, I swear I hear breathing behind me, but I'm at the rear of our group.

"Tiff, did you hear that?" I tap her on the shoulder to get her attention.

"Hear what, Austria?" she asks, giving me an odd look.

I feel a strange energy but can't make out where it comes from. My blood seems to thicken and thud through my body. I flex my fingers and relax them to keep it flowing. I turn around to see if anyone's there but see no one. I catch a familiar scent, maybe an aftershave. Bill and Tiff are talking about the walls and stairways when I see a shadow pass. I could swear the shadow looks familiar, almost like my father's when we walked to the park in the afternoons when I was a child. I'd always run forward and try to make my shadow taller than his. Eventually, he'd cave in, every time, and put me on his shoulders so I could be taller than him. It wasn't until right before he was gone that my growth spurt hit, and I was almost as tall as him.

"Well, everything seems to be as it had been inside," Bill says, exasperated. "I'm stoked the building appears fine thus far. I've seen some pretty crazy things in my lifetime, but this hits the top of the list."

We continue walking around as he tests every load-bearing beam. The electronic gizmo he holds turns green with each test. Tiff and I don't follow when he goes to the basement to assess the structure there. It's weird watching him descend the stairs, like a premonition of him going somewhere, and he won't be returning. I almost ask him to come back when Tiff backslaps my arm. She's pointing down the hall we just walked through, where a vent cover hangs down, flapping precariously. As I walk to inspect it, a numbing sensation spreads through my body. Another unexplainable happening: the vent was fine when we walked by on our way to the basement.

Bill returns with a bewildered look, "The structure appears to be sound. Let's just put the props over by the open wall in the inventory room and hang the costumes the best we can. It's going to take us at least a couple hours to manage that."

We both give him bewildered looks of our own, pointing to the hanging cover. He checks the screws and the frame. As he returns the vent cover to its rightful place, he says, "Would you two mind getting started on the costumes while I check all of the other registers?"

We have to make so many trips back outside that I lose count. I keep getting those feelings of energy, but since Bill and Tiff don't say anything, I don't mention it. I've always seemed to be able to sense more than others, so it's probably nothing. It's just a little annoying to have to flex and unflex my joints to keep my blood flowing.

##

Tiff and I go to a nearby restaurant, Novel, for dinner afterward to unwind. We often get discounts if not free meals because of Tiff's ties to the restaurant industry. She doesn't just work at the haunted house but also for one of the popular restaurants in the city, Flying Saucer. Novel is lit softly and romantically, with an almost orange glow, so a calm feeling settles over me. I order the fried duck neck with curry, smoked raisins and eggplant. Tiff gives me a look of distaste as she orders her broccoli salad; I wonder if she'll leave on the anchovy. I've always had an eclectic palate, having grown up with uncommon food. Even if we were low on money, my parents found ways to keep variety in our meals. My mother stuck to this tradition like a drill sergeant after my father passed away. I recall this morning's memory of him. My chest aches just thinking about him, so I need to think about something else.

"Do you know all the employees this year, Tiff?" I ask.

"I know most of them. Some work with me or in restaurants nearby. There are always a few bussers and hosts looking to make some extra cash. There'll also be Matt, Luke, and Ed. They're part of a fraternity that throws awesome parties."

Tiff sticks out her tongue and holds up hand horns. Then she chugs her water and slams down the glass, rubbing her mouth with the back of her forearm. She holds fisted hands up in celebration. She looks just like a fraternity guy from the movies. She's been taking an acting course this summer with the UMKC Theatre program, and her abilities continue to grow.

"And there are the street kids that Bill employs, hoping to give them enough money to survive the winter," she continues. "Not having a home during the winter in this city can be difficult. In fact, the gatherings at the haunted house are sometimes more of a holiday party than they'll see all year."

I'm happy for the diversion from my previous thoughts. Cliques seem to be growing within the states. At first, I thought it was just something I experienced as part of my high school life, but Mom has noticed the same thing. The states seem to be on the verge of war, and people are becoming polarized. Since funding from the federal government no longer exists, there've been more and more state boundary restrictions.

"So are Matt, Luke, and Ed nice? They sound like they might be ostentatious."

"Oh, they're all right. Just don't let them get to you. Last year they threw mock blood at twenty customers. While they reached their goal of scaring the tar out of them, the customers weren't thrilled about their ruined clothes."

"What did Bill do? I'm surprised they're working here again after that."

"Bill made them work without a paycheck until the cost of replacement clothes was paid. Their parents give money to the haunted house, so they think they can get away with anything."

"I wonder if they'll try a similar trick again this year?"

"Knowing them, they'll probably attempt an even bigger thrill. I'd keep my distance from them if I were you, Austria."

"What about the street kids?"

"Oh, that will probably be Joshua, Ethan, Ceresa, and Patrice. They're kind of intimidating at first, but cool once you get to know them. I tried to offer them jobs at the restaurant last year, but they shot me down. Some of their parents are alcoholics, so they don't like to be around liquor. The others seem to want to find a way on their own."

Our food arrives; my fried duck sizzles and the delicate, natural aroma of eggplant fills my nose. There are extra vegetables on top of that steam. My first bite, full of flavors, sends my taste buds into a frenzy. I'm starving after all our work today, so I have no problem putting this food away. It's also nice to be distracted from not only my heartbreaking memories, but the jitters I'm suffering from thinking about working with people I've never met before.

We're both exhausted and head to our apartment right after dinner. I close my eyes as soon as my head hits the pillow but toss and turn as doubts enter my head. I've always done well at school but have never belonged to a social clique. Tiff's my closest friend. I'm nervous to be stepping outside of my box by taking this job with the haunted house. Will I be able to act well

enough to scare people? That comes naturally to Tiff, but not me. I enjoy writing but
have never done well with drawing or dec-
orations. Beyond that, I find it hard to
fathom not having a home. The street kids
usually find a place to stay, but their num-
bers seem to be increasing lately. A couple
of times I've spotted kids my age sleeping
under bridges. Also, I've never hung out
with fraternity boys, so I'm not sure if I will
fit in at all.

All this is secondary to the fear I have
of the building itself. What was that energy
I sensed? Why did I see shadows no one
else seemed to notice? The shadow appeared almost to be following me specifically. How peculiar, and why did it remind
me of something familiar? I haven't en-
countered that one before. Tomorrow's the
first day for everyone else. I have to get
some rest, so I get up to get a drink of water
and read one chapter of *The Catcher in the
Rye*; this always soothes me. I remember
my father reading children's books to me

when I was little. I would always find a way
to fit on his lap.

INFLUX

At dawn's break, Tiff and I walk in through the huge doors again. The air's hot and musty even this early in the morning, but I don't sense the same energy I did yesterday. I catch a breath of relief, like surfacing from the water when a dive has lasted too long. The morning light shines on the ancient organ in the middle of the main entrance. It's taller than us and dominates the room. I picture my mother sitting on its bench entertaining people in this very building; I can hear Bach's Goldberg Variations bouncing off the walls. We begin to walk to the inventory room where the initiation meeting is to take place. We pass half-lit rooms that'll be constructed into scary scenes. According to Tiff, when fall rolls around and Halloween nears these buildings transform into the "Depths of Hell," "Ghost Riders" and other terror-inspiring names. People of all kinds will line the halls seeking a thrill and this year it's going to stay open all year long.

Three huge guys jump around the corner as we enter the next hall. All of a sudden, my mind warps into thoughts of what these guys have done. I see two of them beating someone into unconsciousness. My perceptions usually don't pick up on people until I've known them for a while. I'm not sure what to make of them as my heart jumps, and I can tell by the look on Tiff's face she's scared, too, but then she smiles. More images of carnage enter my head, but I don't want these people to think I'm a freak when they meet me, so I attempt to stifle them.

"You boys always start spooking early."

"Ah, what's the matter, Tiff," says the blond guy with a sinister smirk.

"Hoping Bill will forgive you for your mistake last year and just pay you with a case of beer this time?"

"Who said it was a mistake, sweetheart?" asks the guy with darker hair and a thicker build.

These must be the Frats: Matt, Ed, and Luke.

"Matt, this is Austria," Tiff says to the blond guy.

"Ready to scare the piss out of some people?" he asks as he offers his hand to shake. He has a square jaw, long, thin nose, and piercing green eyes. I shake his hand firmly the way my father taught me when I was twelve and look straight into his eyes.

"Bet I can do better than you."

Where'd that come from? Last night I was worried sick about my abilities, and now I'm making wagers on whom I can out-scare. He chuckles a bit and lowers his eyebrows at Tiff with a twitch in his left cheek.

"Austria, this is Ed," she says as she turns to the next guy.

"Glad to have another hot chick on board." He offers me his hand to shake too.

"I don't see how looks help when we're hidden behind costumes."

I also shake his hand, but he tries to tug me to him. I twist my wrist so my thumb's between his thumb and forefinger and pull my hand free. He has puppy-dog eyes and beautiful lips that I'm sure most girls find attractive. I stare him down with pursed lips as if to say, "Don't try that move again." I notice the third guy give a smug grin to condone my fleeing his friend's move.

"Ah, and Austria, this is Luke."

"Hi." Luke, the third guy, has a warm smile and the skin around his eyes wrinkles. His handshake is firm but soft too. How does he survive hanging around the other two?

"Nice to meet you," I say. I notice Tiff's eyes linger on Luke a little too long.

Perhaps she has feelings for him. Of the three, she's made a wise choice, if she does.

Tiff and I walk ahead of the group to the meeting, and when we pass the darkest hallway, a cold breeze blows our hair to the side. For a second, I fear I haven't escaped the shadows from yesterday. As my eyes adjust and I glance down the hallway, I see two boys and two girls appear out of the dark. The tattered clothes they wear make me assume they're the street kids.

"Bah, look what the cat drug in," Matt says as he rolls his eyes.

I can't help but stare. I can't even imagine what their lives must be like. I'm half afraid, and half intrigued. I notice a swagger in their walk as they approach us, like they've travelled a world none of us have.

"See you rats mustered up the courage to return," says the guy with dark hair, dark eyes, and matching dark circles under his eyes. "Name's Ethan," he says, tilting his head up to me.

I nod my chin up too, but don't say my name as I'm interrupted.

"Look, you even brought a new one." The two girls smile at each other and then look at me as if there's a hidden joke. They both have cocky smiles and daring eyes. One has tattoos everywhere—on her arms, her neck, and even her hands. The other has one eyebrow with a more angular curve than the other, giving her a look of natural dominance.

"Fresh meat," they say as their smiles fade and their eyes stare me down.

"She's with me, not fresh meat!" Tiff attempts to mediate the situation like she has numerous times among restaurant employees and students at school.

My heart rate jumps, but if I wimp out now, they'll always think I'm a coward. I stand tall.

"So is there any truth to the rumors about this place being actually haunted?" I smile at them. That wasn't really how my mother explained it, but close enough.

Even though it's hard for me to imagine being without a home, I'm very close to someone who once was. My mother was forced to live on the streets for some time with my father before I was born. One of the shelters they stayed in was here.

"How do you know about that?" The girls have lost their proud looks and almost replace them with ones of astonishment.

"Name's Austria. My mother lived here some growing up."

"Hola, I'm Patrice," says the girl with a slanted eyebrow. "And this is Ceresa," she continues as she points to the girl with the tattoos beside her. "And this is Joshua." She points to the one I haven't met. Joshua seems to just kick some dust on the floor, not exactly paying attention. His eyelashes are so long that when he looks up from the ground at me his lashes touch his eyebrows. Then he smiles and hands me a much-needed flashlight. He's blessed with a perfect smile.

From what Tiff has told me, there are Frats, Norms like us, and Streets, and an understood rule that no one dates the other side. So why am I allowing myself to focus on Joshua's lashes and smile?

He keeps looking at me. I wonder if he's noticing how scrawny I am or how long my nose is. I do have some muscle, but with my height it's spread thin. People say I have a pretty smile, and my father always told me that my eyes were full of light, but I think that was just because he was my father. Why does Josh keep staring at me? He hasn't said a word. His face is cut with sharp yet smooth edges at the same time, and his eyes penetrate into me. I breathe and try to slow my heart rate. He wears ragged clothes and a leather jacket regardless of the warmth. He seems to be hesitant or afraid of something.

Then he looks at me and speaks, "Austria, your eyes are gorgeous." He pulls on my sleeve and points me the way we're to go next.

My heart sinks to my stomach. I signed up for this job to figure out what I want to do in life and for a possible trip down my father's memory lane. I did not sign up for a romance, but if he keeps looking at me like that, I'm doomed. Romance doesn't work for me. At least the only relationship I had in high school didn't. We got along in the beginning, but once our relationship grew, he wanted to control my every move, and I felt suffocated.

Well signed up for or not, Joshua excites me. I just need to show him that I make the decisions here. So I do the only thing I can think of. I grab his face, land a peck kiss on his cheek, and walk off. I feel like an idiot, but oh well, too late now.

##

As we get closer to the inventory room, my heart rate won't slow down. There's a wall with vanity after vanity that makes me pause a moment because they're so beautiful. They all must be at least fifty years old. These must have been covered with sheets yesterday—I'd wondered what they were. Now they have occupants sitting and trying to perfect horror makeup in their mirrors. In the center is a circle of boxes, fold-up chairs, and a few old wooden chairs that must have survived with the building itself. I wonder if Bill worked all night preparing this. I hope someone helped him. Then I see the wall with hanging costumes. There are more rollaway racks than I remember. There have to be at least six now, when yesterday we only had three.

I walk over to them and start running my fingers over the costumes one by one. I walk halfway through one when his fingers touch mine. Joshua's calloused fingers brush over my hand. The touch sends a jolt of electricity that arches my spine back. It's like walking into a club where the base shakes your rib cage, uncontrollable. My fingers tingle where they touch his. Joshua looks like a nightmare I should run from, but I can't resist his pull. I put my hand on his shoulder to balance myself and keep him at a distance.

"I go by Josh, not Joshua," he says, just now correcting the introduction from the hallway. "So, which costume's your favorite?"

"I would have to say the female vampire that's crimson and black, full length with a gap at the stomach and a low neckline, but conservative enough to be tasteful. It almost has a *Phantom of the Opera* verve. I just adore the neck of the cape that's raised to the hairline. Something about it frightens you while drawing you in at the same time."

He doesn't answer at first. Probably thinks I'm an off-balance woman to go on so much about a silly costume. Then he looks at me.

"I think I know precisely what you mean."

He gives me a sideways smile, and I know I'm in trouble. Look at those eyes.

They're blue as the sea, but you can see the
sand at the bottom they are so clear.

ASSIGNMENTS

Bill hands everyone a piece of paper.

"I've assigned you all a team. I'm tired of you picking your own group. Our haunted rooms need variety. You know the rules. No fighting, and if you damage anything you pay for it. Now, read your papers. Team Exodus, please stand by the vanities, Team Sinister by the props, Team Decapitation by the rollaway racks, and Team Mummified here in the center."

I feel like I've been either handed a legal sentence or a winning lottery ticket. Who will be on my team? I slowly unfold the paper. Team Exodus with Ceresa, tattoo lady; Matt, scary blond; and Jack, a boy I haven't personally met, but recognize as a busser at Tiff's restaurant. Wonderful. Matt's the most intimidating to me of the three college guys, and Ceresa looks like she doesn't fear anything.

I breathe in through my nose and out my mouth to calm myself down. I head over to the vanities and watch the others to see what team they're on. Tiff heads to the props to be part of Team Sinister. So does Ed, Matt's sidekick, Ethan, the scariest of the street kids, and Lea, a girl I haven't met, who works at Tiff's restaurant as a hostess. Well, so far Bill seems to be meeting his goal of diversity. I guess Tiff being with Lea is somewhat breaking that mold, but Tiff's an actress and maybe Lea isn't.

Then I look toward the rollaway racks to see Team Decapitation and see Josh heading to them. Patrice comes up behind him and hooks her arm in his. I can't help clenching my hands into fists. Bill missed the variety there. Obviously two street kids put together will overrule the others. If I weren't new to this, I'd file a complaint with Bill. Since me working here is kind of a favor, I don't really have much of an option but to bear the hooked arms. Maybe my mother was right about working here not being a good idea. Luke and a guy I don't recognize head there too. Four more people I don't recognize gather in the center to form Team Mummified. Bill clears his throat.

"Flip your papers over and you'll see the map of the haunted house. The room you'll be in is highlighted. Your scripts are at your current stations."

Ceresa picks up a stack of pages, takes one, and hands the rest to Matt. He takes a page and then hands me the remaining. As his hand reaches out to me, a shadow races across the room and the makeup brush on the vanity next to me falls to the floor. For some reason, the scene from *Ghost,* when Patrick Swayze is finally able to lift a penny to show Demi Moore he's there, surfaces in my brain. Jack, who is standing on my other side, jumps, startled. I wonder how long he's going to last at the haunted house. Crap. The shadows are back. I push the thought from my head, hoping the others don't notice how much the shadow has shaken me. They'll probably assume something innocent knocked over the brush. But I can't stop my blood from feeling like molasses through my veins.

"Well, that was weird," I say as I hand the last page to Jack, attempting to cover my anxiety. With big eyes, he grabs it. Jack's a sweet-looking kid. He has full cheeks like a child. He must have a growth spurt left in him.

We're Team Exodus, so it fits that our room has different groups that have moved en masse. Oppressed people pushed to suicide in Jonestown, the hundreds of movement brothers to be executed in Egypt, and slaves leaving their rulers after a plague. My mind begins reeling with ideas. I feel creativity blossoming from within. This is one of the reasons I signed up. I think my father would be proud of me. The story of his life seems like somewhat of a letdown when told by others. I know there has to be more to it. I hope I can find it here.

"We should get the props set up first. What would work for the cyanide? How do you set up a fake hanging? How do we make a scene of back in Moses' time?" I ask.

The script says that we'll have someone offering candy "cyanide" pills to customers that an employee also consumes followed by the employee dropping in what looks like the death throes of poisoning. My knowledge of toxicity is limited. I can't believe I'm getting paid for this. It's going to be a blast.

"Whoa! Don't you like taking charge?" Matt asks.

"Got any better idea where to begin?" Ceresa counters.

I smile at her, and she bumps into my arm with a smile as we walk to the props. Okay, so not as frightening as the tattoos had built up in my head. Jack kneels next to a silver platter perfect to hold the "cyanide." Now that's just creepy. Bill walks up to us.

"There's already candy set up in your room. That tray's an excellent choice for the finishing touch for Jonestown Massacre. Good eye, Jack."

Jack blushes as he smiles. Maybe he'll last longer than I thought.

I imagine someone falling over in convulsions, customers believing they're poisoned. It's simply sheer magic.

"I'm Jim Jones, right?" Matt insists.

"Of course, your personality fits that of a reverend," I answer sarcastically.

"Who's my victim?"

"According to the scripts it's me but don't think you're getting out of it." Ceresa balks as she looks up from her page.

"She's right. Reverend Jones dies of a headshot wound."

This comes from little Jack, and I have to hide my smile. He seems like someone I would've liked to have as a little brother if my father had lived longer and he and my

mother could've had more children. I can
see the fear in Matt's eyes. Not as tough as
I thought either. Bill's shaking his head.
Guess the mix of people in the group is
bound to give him a headache. He starts to
say something. Probably to remind us that
the first rule is to not fight, but he isn't able
to begin. Next to us at the costumes Ethan
shoves Luke. Luke's ready to shove him
back when Bill races to them and breaks it
up. Now Bill will be able to remind everyone, and not just us, that no fighting is allowed.

"Quit it. If you can't find a way to get
along, I'll have to ask you to leave."

"He shoved me," Luke says. "It would
be only fair for me to shove him back. You
always give them more leeway."

"Oh yeah, so much leeway," Ethan
says. "In order to stay here last night, we
had to set up the rest of the costumes. The
only reason that executioner costume you
were arguing with me for is here is because

I worked to set it out. Rat, you should be grateful that all I did was shove you."

I guess that answers my question as to whether Bill had help setting up everything else—the street kids.

At this, Luke doesn't have a counter for Ethan, so he hands him the costume.

"Yeah, but Luke's part of Team Decapitated, so it seems fitting for him to have the costume," Tiff argues.

"Actually, Austria's going to wear that one when she hangs Jack. Look at it. It's too small for either of you," Bill answers.

Ethan brings me the costume.

"Look forward to seeing it on you," he says to me.

I just take it from him and turn away. I catch Josh sneering at him, and my heart flutters.

"Okay, everyone take turns grabbing props you need and move them to the room for setup. Then I'll go room to room and help you. Team Exodus will go first as you have already begun."

We have the tray, rope for the hanging, and some rods such as might have been used in the Moses era. We grab those and leave to head to our room. The halls are dark. I'm overwhelmed with a sense of foreboding as if I'm being spied on. It's exhaustive enough to navigate the dark halls even with Bill's map. I find myself steadying the rhythm of my breaths yet again. My foot hits something, and I trip. I would've fallen, but Ceresa catches me.

"Did your mom not tell you about those? These are the tunnels the employees use to move from room to room unseen by the customers. The builders didn't close up all of the walls, so some of the supports jut out. Better watch out for them. I'm not always going to be around to catch you."

She shakes her head, but I can see a smile tugging at the corner of her mouth. I feel the kindness in the advice she gives me even though she sees it as an unwanted responsibility. It makes me feel more like I belong here, like she's an older sibling, and

I'm the brat little sister. I begin to wonder if Ceresa, one of the scariest to me when I first met her, might become a close friend. Then we enter the room nearest to the haunted house entrance. Bill's already in the room. Matt and Jack begin to place the candies on the tray. Bill checks to be sure none will fall off if the tray were to be tilted. Ceresa eats one, and after a few seconds falls to the floor, her body shaking spastically. Matt then acts out the suicidal shot to his head. He holds his index finger and thumb to mimic a gun. It appears we forgot a prop.

"Now Jack, step over here and try on this harness. We're going to have you hanging from this. The background here hides the wires that will hold you up. Austria, you'll put a noose on him for his hanging. Then you'll kick the chair out from under him. Jack must do some acting to make it appear as though he's choking."

Jack puts the harness on with an excited look. There's a belt that wraps beneath his shirt as well as shoulder straps. He'll have a specially made shirt when we go live. He steps up onto a chair. Bill adjusts the harness so that none of Jack's body weight is on the chair. I step up onto a small platform next to them. Bill shows me how to loosen and tighten the noose. It all seems pretty easy. I just have to do this placing my hands naturally around the wires holding him up. I put the loop around Jack's head, and it lies on his shoulders. Jack looks at me, and I struggle to tighten the noose. I can't bring myself to do it. I hate death. My mother has consoled me an infinite number of times over my father's death. Maybe I didn't fully think out this job.

"Are you sure the harness will hold him, Bill?"

"Yeah, it can hold a person my weight, and I weigh much more than Jack here."

"Okay."

I swallow and apprehensively move the knot. It's tight on Jack's neck now.

"His hands and legs will be tied when we're live," Bill informs us.

"Kick the chair now, Austria."

I think Ceresa's trying to coach or cheer me, but it isn't helping. I breathe in through my nose, close my eyes, breathe out, and open them. I kick the chair hard, and it slides two feet. Jack's body begins shaking, and his face turns bright red. He appears to be in agony. I grab him and raise him a couple inches. Everyone laughs at me.

"Good acting, kid. You'll have to control yourself from trying to save him when customers are around, Austria."

I should feel mortified, but I find myself proud of the kid for proving my initial impression of him wrong and being talented at this haunted house gig. Matt gives Jack a high five. I guess I shouldn't have worried about the kid surviving at all. I probably should be more worried about myself. I bet he acts with Tiff. She should've given me a heads up. I'm pretty embarrassed, but that only lasts a second.

Bill's walking us to the final part of our room. It guides the customers to the hallway that leads to the next section.

"Ceresa, you'll lead the customers. You will have this staff and be dressed for the time. You'll say that Moses has split the sea, and they must hurry."

Just then Bill flips a switch and the wall surrounding the doorway fills with what looks like blue water with some kind of light causing it to glow, the doorway splitting the current. I don't know how he put this together, but it's amazing. I didn't expect to be so enamored with the creativity of the haunted house. The careful detail Bill has put into the place is moving. His technique impresses me.

"How did you do this?" I ask.

"It's just two panes of glass with water between. The hallway's the same way. Now Matt, there's a chariot and costume in the corner. You'll chase the customers to the next room. You'll wear goggles with glowing red eyes."

"Sweet."

"All right, you all go back to the inventory room. I hear Tiff's restaurant snuck in some good grub. Practice your lines. Work on finishing touches for makeup. Stay out of trouble. I need to work with Team Sinister now."

I can smell the food as we walk back. I'm so hungry that I almost feel like running. I hear people talking and laughing. I can't help but smile. Strangely enough, I'm enjoying this, the adrenaline rush of a scare, pushing myself to new experiences. As we enter, I see Josh and Luke surprisingly holding what seems to be an exciting discussion. Ceresa jumps next to them.

"So where's the food, boys? I'll torture you if there isn't anything good left."

"Oh, don't get your panties in a knot. The food's right over there on the boxes by the chairs in the center."

I'm afraid Luke doesn't realize how hungry we are. Ceresa stomps one foot right next to his and pushes her face quickly toward his. She's taunting him, but he just smiles. He softly puts his hands on her shoulders and turns her around.

"Would you like ketchup on your hamburger, babe?"

Ceresa is about to elbow him in the side when her eyes catch the food. She just smiles and runs to it. There are to-go boxes with labels. Hamburger and fries, turkey wrap, chicken tenders, and veggie burgers. The smells from the boxes make my mouth water. Each person from our team grabs a box and takes a seat. Pretty soon, everyone in the room joins our little gathering. It's nice to see such a mix of people sharing a meal and conversation together. I think this must have been what Bill was after. There's a warm feeling in my chest—a feeling of belonging that I never expected.

Josh sits next to me. He smiles and watches everyone too.

"Pretty cool, huh. Ever think you'd be hanging out with some street-kids and enjoy it?"

I smile at him and move a piece of hair that has fallen into his eyes. We freeze. Then Team Sinister enters the room with Bill.

"Okay, grab yourselves some food. We'll all take a short break. Teams Decapitation and Mummified will go over their rooms this afternoon, and then we'll be done for the day."

Team Sinister begins grabbing boxes of food.

"Oh, here, Tiff. They said this one's for you. Said it's your favorite," Ed says.

"Get out. That's awesome."

Tiff goes to Ed and grabs the box. Something bothers me about this scenario, but I'm not able to say anything before she opens the box. Tiff's scream is the highest pitched sound I have ever heard. She drops the box. It's full of wiggly worms that begin to crawl out of the box.

"Booyah!" says Ed.

"Pick up that box, Ed, and get it out of here. There better not be a worm left in this place," Bill scolds.

"If he misses a worm you should make him eat it, Bill," Patrice adds.

Nice to see Patrice sticking up for Tiff, but I wish Ed and Matt would give it a break already. Maybe someone should help them do that. A plan begins to formulate in my head.

"Tiff, Patrice, Ceresa, can you help me figure out the makeup? I've never used theatrical makeup before."

They head over to the vanities with me. Ceresa whispers first.

"You got a plan, Austria?"

I'm a little taken aback by her willingness to side with me. I'm unsure if it's a feminist move or if she's just tired of seeing the fraternity guys pick on everyone. A wave of self-confidence flows through me as I answer.

"Not exactly, but those guys can't get away with this," I can't help the crooked smile that forms on my face. It feels good to take charge.

Patrice grabs some makeup and begins applying it to my face to keep up pretenses.

"Remember last year, Tiff?" Patrice asks.

"Yeah, what about it?"

"Matt and Ed were in the inventory room and you snuck up on them with the *Scream* mask. Ed grabbed Matt's arm, and they both yelled like little girls. I've never seen those two spooked before, but something about that mask gets to them."

"You're right. Do we have any left?"

"We have four and, so far, they're not needed for any of the rooms."

"That's good. We should all have one and torment them with them until they're done picking on everyone else. Give them a dose of their own medicine."

I'm ecstatic. I can tell all four of us are filled with anticipation. I wonder if Patrice and Ceresa will be friends with me like this outside of the haunted house. What would the kids from my high school, who are pretty much all going to college, think if we went to lunch and a couple street girls approached? I would set them straight. They seem all too comfortable in their collegiate surroundings. It's like they could be happy their entire lives surrounded by only a certain type of person. The thought's utterly ridiculous. We get only one life in this world, why spend it in only one circle? If I ever marry someone like that, I would find myself bored after a year. My mother married a man with an open mind.

INCEPTION

Bill calls out to everyone, his voice reaching for us all like the fingers of a fog's mist. "That's a wrap, for tonight at least. Everyone go and get some rest, come in with fresh minds and more ideas to work in the light tomorrow. Have a good evening and stay out of trouble."

Everyone gathers to their normal groups and disperses. Tiff and I head out the door to go grab some decaffeinated coffee and discuss today's happenings before going to bed. I notice Josh running up behind us, an electric wave surpassing its perimeter. Guess we won't be discussing that one.

"Uh, hello, did I forget something back there?" I ask.

"No, not at all. Can I join you beautiful ladies? Wouldn't want you to roam the streets at this hour without a guard," Josh says.

Tiff begins to turn him down when I interrupt.

"That sounds like a good idea, Josh," I say.

I can't ignore Tiff's look of skepticism, the panic in her eyes. Broadway Café is reasonably busy at this time of night, a studious and companionable atmosphere on a caffeinated buzz. Some sit alone at a laptop or reading a book. Others are in groups talking or playing chess. We all sit and discuss our rooms and teams over coffee like we're haunting pros. The seats are comfortable, and the ones we're in are upholstered in velvet. We have also been on our feet most of the past couple days. It is exceptional. Though so comfortable and tired, I have not felt this alive in a long time. Tiff excuses herself after the first round. I can see that she is tired, maybe a little disappointed by the way she narrows her eyes at me. I'm sure we'll have a discussion about this later.

I turn back to Josh and find his gaze into my eyes to be all-consuming. He grabs my hands and asks, "Please tell me you feel the electricity between us and I'm not just imagining this all in my head."

I am so shocked that my breath hitches. He feels it too and what he describes is very similar to how I've explained it in my head, electricity. It's a tingling feeling, as if we're pulled together by something stronger than ourselves, but I'm not ready to tell him that.

"Maybe I do and maybe I don't," I say.

He gasps, "Yeah?" then half laughs, half clears his throat before continuing. "I once visited The Magic House in St. Louis and they had an exhibit with an electricity charged ball that made your hair stand on end. It's like that first second when you touch the ball, and the electricity shoots through you."

We both take a deep breath and stare at each other.

I have to focus deeply to gulp and regroup. He has to know I feel the same way. I've been unable to control my blushing when he's around.

I want to ask Josh about himself. This I am dying to know, but I can tell he's hesitant, so I start with myself. I pull my jacket sleeves over my hands nervously.

"I grew up poor but always with a roof over my head. My father died a few years ago. My mother says it was something from back on the streets that caught up with him. She hasn't told me much about living on the streets but enough to know it wasn't easy. I'm working to decide what I want to do with my life. I dream of being able to provide for her when she's older and for my own family. I love to write, but I'm torn because that doesn't always pay the bills."

There's a small silence, and then he speaks. He's spinning a butter knife between his index finger and the table.

"Life has been hard for me since I can remember. I do live on the streets and always have. Both my parents are gone. I just take it one day at a time. I love to draw."

He grabs my hands gently and pulls them toward him so that I'm facing him. "You take my breath away," he says.

I'm locked as if nothing else exists. I lean into him and peck kiss him. He grabs my chin and answers back with more passion. The electricity I'm feeling must be sending sparks shooting from me. I take a deep breath as he releases me. He's looking out the window at something and moves to shield me from whatever is outside. I wonder what he sees. Whatever it is, it seems to have interrupted us. What if it was his ex-girlfriend or something?

"I'll walk you home," he says. "I wasn't joking about it not being safe for you to be out here at this hour."

I just grab his hand and pull him close. The air has a slight chill to it, but part of that's my psychological fear of rejection. Did he feel the sparks I felt or am I totally deranged? It seems as if he's fleeing that moment, our kiss, now and I want to cling to him in hopes we can kiss again.

As we approach my place, he grabs my chin again to look at my eyes. He has tears in his. Where did this come from? He must have felt the sparks and feared rejection more than I did. I'm not used to seeing emotion like this from a guy. I wonder if it's just Josh himself or a trait he may have picked up living in the streets. I would think the streets would do the opposite and harden him. He kisses my forehead, and I hug him before letting go. It feels as if he believes this isn't possible. What he needs is someone to believe in him, and I will if he'll let me. I believe, I cannot accurately feel this quite yet... that I will love him completely one day. Perhaps my perceptions are right. I need a different artistic light to my days that he, I know, would bring to me. I need someone who will take me for how I am and not try to change me to fit in their little trophy case on their mantel. And then he releases me, and the distance in his eyes has me running up the steps to my apartment without looking back. He just stares down the street. This is extremely confusing. I don't understand his volatile demeanor.

"So…how'd it go, Austria?" Tiff asks as I close the door. I'm looking out the front window watching him run down the street in the same direction he's been staring. His strides are beautifully paced like a swimmer, but so smooth, he doesn't make a splash.

"Pretty good."

"That's it. Pretty good. You're boringly vague."

"No, I mean not just pretty good, but fabulous. We kissed, Tiff, but then it was intensely awkward. It was like he wasn't really that into it. He was just staring out the window."

"What was he staring at?"

"I don't know. Does it matter?"

"Well, maybe. Go on."

"He just seemed very hot one second and cold the next. Have you noticed anything off about him?"

"Um, no. Josh is balanced. I think I know why he might have been distracted. Did anything else happen?"

"We hugged goodnight and he got distracted at the end of that too. Maybe he decided part way through the kiss that he's just not that interested in me. After the hug, he just kept staring down the street. I don't remember seeing anything that stood out."

I try to recollect every detail of the evening to see if I overlooked anything. The first thought that comes to mind is how Josh smelled of woods and rain. He didn't reek of body odor the way some guys our age can. He smelled as if he took a nap in a forest. That memory isn't going to help me figure out what I need to identify. What was on the street? The bubbly atmosphere in the café was enticing. People seemed in their element there. Beyond them was the night outside. Then I peel back the layers of excitement I'd felt in Josh's company, and there was a moment of darkness that washed over me before he looked away. I do remember a few other faces looking outside when Josh had been. I remember seeing the rear of a vehicle peeling out, a Range Rover. At our house, I saw similar taillights. That has to be it.

"I noticed taillights belonging to a Range Rover," I say.

"Shoot. That means they've found us. They know where we live."

"What are you talking about, Tiff?"

"Matt and Ed drive a Range Rover. They seem just like jokesters, but their fun doesn't stop there. Two years ago, they beat Josh so bad he had a concussion."

I guess their opulent appearance is just a cover for their snarling and hateful true selves. My initial read upon meeting them had been right on.

"Oh no. So were they watching us tonight? What do they plan to do?"

"It sounds like they more than likely were," Tiff says. "We'll have to get an alarm system on the house and always walk in at least pairs if not groups outside. Poor Josh, they can find him in any old abandoned building he sleeps in. Hopefully, Ethan will be with him, or he can stay with Bill."

"I hope so," I say. I can't shake the images of Matt and Ed attacking. "Why did they do that to Josh?"

"Josh's the one who shone the spotlight on them when they dropped mock blood on the customers. Had he not done that, they would have probably gotten away with it. Instead the customers were able to easily identify their assailants. Don't worry, Austria. Diesel will be our guard tonight. He'll be on them in a second if they ever invade our home."

Tiff scratches behind Diesel's ear. He's a good dog, and I'm glad we have him even more so now. I sit beside them and start scratching behind his other ear. His tail begins wagging immediately.

"Sounds good, Tiff. You should've warned me about more of this before we began at the haunted house."

"I was hoping it wouldn't come up. Would it have stopped you?"

"No. I've enjoyed the experience. It's brought me out of my slump. We should probably get to bed if we want to be of any use tomorrow."

We both head to bed. I wonder if I'm going to have another restless night.

I shouldn't have wondered. I knew. I toss and turn. One nightmare that jars me awake tonight is of Matt and Ed in dark hoods surprising Josh in his sleep in a dusty, abandoned building by beating on him with objects I cannot make out. In my dream I run to interfere but am quickly knocked unconscious. It's weird to have a dream within a dream, but that is what I believe I'm having now. I see Matt and Ed doing something more cynical than in my initial dream. They're with a group of men looking at blueprints, but then something blocks my perceptive ability like when I'd been holding the costume outside the haunted house. I read another chapter and go back to sleep. I'm thankful to fall to sleep easily this time. It seems as if the next dream begins the second my head hits the pillow. I hear my father's voice.

"Ready or not, here I come."

I'm hiding inside our hexagon table. The one fully enclosed with two doors that only a preschooler or younger could fit in. I giggle when I hear his footsteps in the room. He's unsuccessful in his first few attempts to find me, so I allow myself to giggle again, louder this time. I hear his footsteps approach and then the doors open. He smells of his aftershave, a hint of ocean breeze. His eyes light up as he smiles at me. He gently holds my hand as I crawl out. Then he scoops me up and holds me in his arms. I nuzzle my nose into the nape of his neck, where the smell of his aftershave is the strongest. He pulls his head back to take a look at me.

"Good hiding, kid. You're growing too fast. Now it's my turn to hide."

He sets me down, and I begin to count.

My alarm goes off, and the sun peeks through my curtains. Guess the dream put me into a restful sleep. I wish I could've stayed in the dream with my father. I miss him so much it hurts, and I always feel like there's a void in my life without him.

ACQUIREMENT

The next day we're introduced to the three rooms that still need creating. No scene or plot has been set yet, they're blank canvases. Bill asks for volunteers and my hand shoots up before I'm even aware of it. I catch Josh's sideways smirk as he raises his hand, too. I can't seem to get a good read on him. He hasn't spoken to me all morning. I should've just steered clear of guys here altogether. Of course, Tiff's one of my creative muses so she raises her hand too, although I'm beginning to have a feeling that there may be a new muse in my life, or not. Patrice raises her hand. I hope fervently that she isn't Josh's muse, but my fear drops dramatically when I catch Ethan's face out of the corner of my eye. He raises his hand, looks at Patrice quickly, and then looks away, attempting to hide his interest. I also see Luke raising his hand while looking at Tiff. When she looks back, a blush appears on his cheeks. Apparently, crossing lines and forming new relation-ships must be catching. I'm even more sur-prised when Matt and Ed raise their hands. Of course, Matt would want to show that he can haunt better than the rest of us. If he only knew he doesn't stand a chance. Knowing what I do now about Matt and Ed, I want to get them back even more than be-fore.

"Okay, Ethan, Patrice, Matt, and Ed are in a group together. Josh, Austria, Luke, and Tiff are in the other group. Your sup-plies are in the center of the room," Bill says.

There are large pieces of paper in the center of the circle with markers on top of them. Bill instructs us that there are three papers for each of the unplanned rooms. We're to work on the setting, the lines, and the overall atmosphere of the room. I take a piece of paper, Tiff takes one, and Josh takes one. We walk over to a private corner. As we go by the rollaway racks, Josh looks directly at my favorite vampire costume and then raises his eyebrows at me. Good idea. Josh and I already know what our atmosphere's going to be, but I have to come up with a way so Tiff believes she's the inspiration for this idea as my muse. So I tell her about the attraction I had to the haunted house job when she first told me about it, but about the fright too. I was running a big risk going against my mother's warning. One that may cost me a scholarship, but it could be a step toward the true career I want, to be a fiction writer, a novel writer. It could also bring me closer to my father or at least his memory. While I haven't outwardly declared this as a reason for taking the job, it's probably the most important. I have to fill the void. I don't think I can live another year splintered by the pain of his loss. I hope to find closure here.

Josh looks at me and just says, "Interesting."

The atmosphere in our room is to be one of alluring danger that draws in its prey, like a vampire. We'll have a child in one corner that appears afraid. I write out the lines here. Josh draws the scene. He's an amazing artist. The pictures are remarkably intricate—I can see a tiny tear beginning to drop from the child's eye. Tiff acts it out for us so we can see loose ends or where one train of thought might not work and needs reorganizing. It's funny watching her switch from role to role. I almost laugh when she changes from a woman to a boy. After the customers are scared by monsters while trying to check on the child, a beautiful woman will grab their hands and tell them to run this way. She will then be taken down. After that, the customers will have to fend for themselves as they see images of the child and woman being tortured by a monstrous, vampire couple. The winding path will make them nervous and, just as it clears, they will be chased to the exit only to have the risen dead woman and child be behind that door to scare them more. It is epic, and we just slapped it together in five minutes.

Bill walks around handing us maps of where our new rooms will be.

"Just like yesterday, I will walk around to each room to help set up. Everyone who didn't volunteer for one of these rooms will help move props and costumes. If extras are needed, that'll be your responsibility too. Work hard, and we may be able to call it early today."

I already know who our child will be, Jack. At least I already know he's a talented actor, but I'm unsure of how to ask him to play the role of a child without insulting him. He's seventeen but hasn't hit his last growth spurt so can pass as fourteen and after we dress him young, he'll pass for twelve.

"Hey Jack, can you help us set up?"

At least I can get him involved so he hears our script. I'm hoping he'll volunteer for the spot without me having to ask.

Luke and Josh begin gathering the equipment and props we'll need, like a television set and a camera. We can film the images of the woman and child being tortured beforehand and air it when live. We'll need plain, normal clothes for the woman and child before the change. Makeup will be crucial for when they rise from the dead. We'll also need instruments of torture for the attacker.

Tiff gives me a look and nods toward Patrice and Ceresa, who are behind one of the rollaway racks. As I walk their way, Patrice nods in the direction of the only closet in the room. It holds antique furniture that's only to be used with caution. It also currently holds Matt and Ed. Perfect, I think.

When I join the girls, I see what they have behind the rollaway, the *Scream* masks we discussed. Is it bad that I look forward to this little piece of revenge? We all put on the masks and black clothing that disguises any identifiable part—hoodies, gloves, pants and boots —as quickly and quietly as possible. Then head to the closet. Patrice holds a flashlight, Ceresa a pretend knife, and Tiff has one of those voice changers. I wonder if it works. I also wonder if we'll all fit in the closet. Patrice jumps in first, turning off the light and shining the flashlight in Matt and Ed's eyes, blinding them. Ceresa holds the knife in the light as she enters. Tiff talks with that weird anonymous caller voice as Patrice shines the light on Ceresa's mask. I step in last and growl as I close the door. Ceresa advances on Matt with the knife. Matt and Ed scream, which is fabulous. They shove us aside, open the door, and run out. We all fall on each other laughing.

"Not cool. Don't think we won't get you back. You have no idea what we can do."

Ed's trying to threaten us, but it doesn't quite work when he's as white as a sheet.

Matt hasn't said a word and looks like he might be sick. All I can think of is how much fun that was. I can't wait to do it again. What's wrong with me? I like flustering these guys that have been lurking around following me. Hopefully, it will discourage them from more of the same.

"Okay, everybody calm down. You need to save the scaring for paying customers. Do you want to get out early today or what?"

"Sorry, Bill, they deserved it though," Tiff tries to explain as we walk back to our responsibilities. I notice Bill has to cover his mouth to hide a smile. He clears his throat.

"That might be true, but in order to follow the rules and not have anyone hurt, let's not do that again."

I feel bad that Patrice has to work with Matt and Ed now. At least she'll have Ethan with her. Now I see Ceresa is going to join her too. Good. Tiff's heading back to Luke and Josh. Before I turn to do the same, I take one last look at Matt and Ed. They're popping the knuckles on their hands, then they both turn and look directly at me at the same time. Why are they only looking at me? Is it because I'm the new kid? A cold sweat dampens the back of my neck as I turn to walk away.

That's when it happens. Shadows begin to swarm around me. It's like they're circling vultures, and I'm the carcass. The energy makes me as dizzy as if I were dehydrated on a desert. And everything goes black for a second. When it's light again, I'm hovering above everybody. At first, I think I've died and am having an out-of-body experience, but then I hear them. Bill's over my body on one side checking my pulse, and says that I've fainted, embarrassing. Josh and Tiff are on the other side of me and look concerned. Then I hear a voice I would recognize anywhere. When I turn to my right, my voice recognition is confirmed. My father is there. He looks hazy, as if looking at a mirage. He reaches out his hand. I reach out mine. The warmth I feel when I hold his ghostly hand is like a favorite blanket I had as a child. My father looks me in the eyes.

"Be careful, Austria."

He says that like he always did before, but this time the fear in his eyes is deeper, more serious. And then he fades away. I close my eyes, trying to memorize the moment. When I open my eyes, I'm lying on the floor, and everyone's looking at me with worried expressions.

"Austria, are you okay?" Tiff asks.

"Yeah, not sure what that was all about."

"Austria, is there someone we can call? I would like you to see a doctor," Bill says.

"I'm fine, really."

"Oh, come on. You don't want to worry an old man."

"Okay, Tiff can call my mother."

Tiff drives me to the doctor's office, with looks of concern directed at me the entire way. The smell of sanitary cleanser gags me as we enter. It's cold too. My heart palpitates when I see her; my mother's standing in the waiting room checking me in. I can only imagine how furious she is. I wonder how long it will be until she says, "I told you so."

We sit down, and I grab the closest magazine. I don't read anything, just flip through the pages browsing the photos. Tiff explains to my mother what happened.

"We had just played a practical joke on some of the employees at the haunted house and then she fainted. It was weird. It was like the life had left her and then it came back. No one touched her. I don't know what happened."

"Don't worry, sweetie. You did the right thing by calling me and bringing her here."

My mother just sits there staring off into space. I know she wants to ask me a dozen questions. The silence is worse than that. Is she upset that I took the job and might lose a scholarship? Then she looks at me, smiles, and softly presses her hand to my cheek. So maybe she's not mad and just distressed. The doctor calls me in. His name's Dr. Shipley. He's nice enough but distant. He says he wants to run some blood tests. The nurse rubs my arm with an antiseptic wipe. I don't watch when she pricks me with the needle but take a peek when she's swirling the vial of my blood. I experience another cold sweat even though the blood looks normal enough.

Back in the room my mother finally speaks to me.

"Are you feeling all right, Austria?"

"Yes, there's nothing to worry about. I think I just got overwhelmed with excitement is all."

"Well, be sure to stay hydrated and get rest from now on, darling."

"Okay, okay. I'm seventeen years old. I can handle myself."

Doctor Shipley enters just then.

"Hi, Austria. Sounds like you had a bit of a spell earlier today. Could you tell me about it?"

"There's not much to tell. Just overwhelmed."

I don't know why, but I don't feel comfortable telling anyone, even my mother, about the shadows, the out of body experience, or my father. I'm afraid they'll look at me like I'm not thinking straight.

"Well, your blood shows a high healing ability, so that's good."

"What do you mean, high healing ability?" my mother asks the question I'm thinking.

"Austria's blood has stronger DNA than usual. You know, there's been a lot of interesting new studies on DNA in the last few years. Much of what we thought was wasted space in the DNA strand, about 95%, is turning out to be a whole lot more. Instead of wasted space, it's turning out to be wasted potential. You have an Altered Helix. Human beings have always been equipped with all sorts of capabilities that very few of us ever realize, and I think that there just might be more to you than meets the eye, Austria. Of course, nothing in this world is free. Everything comes at a price, and maybe fainting is yours."

I'm not sure what to think of all this. Am I a freak of nature? It all seems subtle. No one would notice the differences in me. People have fainted since the beginning of time. Why does it have to mean that there's something different about me? Doctor Shipley must be able to tell that I'm confused by the look on my face.

"This is nothing to worry about, dear. Most of the time there will be no effects. Just keep hydrated and get some rest."

"That's precisely what I told her."

"You have a smart mother. Stay well."

We leave the room and check out. I notice Doctor Shipley on the phone as we're about to exit.

"It's as expected. Yes, I'll get it to you tonight."

Then he spots me looking at him and covers his mouth with his hand. What was expected and who is he speaking to? Is he talking about me? Did my mother hear him? My mother doesn't ask me questions during the drive as I had imagined. I figured she'd blame this whole thing on the haunted house and tell me, "I told you so." Instead, she hasn't said a word. I don't think she's intentionally giving me the silent treatment, though. I keep catching her chewing on the inside of her lip out of the corner of my eye. She's nervous, but I thought the doctor said it was nothing. Is something going on with my mother that I don't know about? When we are in front of the apartment I share with Tiff, she gives me a hug. I don't think I'm going to get her to open up tonight, but I make a mental note to check in with her later. I try to read into her emotions like I've done before but the flood of images is too much. I don't know why, but I feel nervous for her.

"I love you, Austria."

"I love you too, Mother."

CATECHISM

The next morning, I take a breather and write before going to the haunted house. I always try to draw a cartoon of the scene I'm writing about before I begin, to get the creative juices flowing. It's pretty hilarious to see, since drawing is definitely not one of my talents. Maybe I could turn them into comics to go along with the books. I attempt to draw a cartoon man trying to grab a cartoon woman's hand. I hold up the piece of paper and in actuality it looks as if he's walking her on a leash. My drawing is so awful it turns a romantic scene into S&M. Either way, it has stirred my imagination.

I boot up the laptop and begin typing. I get to a word I know but can't remember how to spell. I instantly miss living with my mother. She's like a dictionary on two legs. Anytime I wrote at our house, I could just say a word like a Spelling-Bee judge, and she'd spout out the letters like a contestant.

It had been just the two of us for the past few years. We had our routines memorized. She used to always have my shoes right by the front door every day, despite my never following her request to put them there. I always made her chamomile tea when we'd curl up on the couch to watch a show before bed. I miss how she would paint my fingernails while we watched a movie. Maybe we can watch a movie sometime after the haunted house preparations are complete.

##

At the haunted house, everyone gives me looks of concern as I enter the inventory room. Luke and Ethan ask me how I'm doing. I assure them it was nothing, and I'm fine. Tiff puts a reassuring hand on my shoulder. Ceresa claps. She and Patrice smile in unison—they're glad I'm okay. Josh doesn't meet my gaze; his face is still as a statue. I'm distraught by his reaction. I notice he's staring Matt and Ed down, but they aren't doing anything. Did they attack Josh again? I wish someone would tell Bill how serious they are. Maybe someone has, but because of the money their parents give, he's too paralyzed to react. If anything, Matt and Ed seem to be focused on only the work for once. They're organizing the rest of the props by rooms so that they can easily be moved to the correct destination. They seem to be efficient and organized. Bill gives them a nod of approval. I notice Ed make eye contact with Josh. Then he looks at me. I raise my eyebrows silently and cock my head to the side, approving of his and Matt's actions. He looks down and shakes his head. He can't even take a compliment. Guess the trick on them just made them hate us more. Are they just trying to butter up Bill with their actions? Why would they care enough? They have to be after something, why can't I figure out what? It's as if the increase of attraction and caring toward Josh is causing me to lose my sense of perception.

I busy myself to keep from feeling so lost. Patrice and Ceresa help me with makeup for real this time. There's no need to plot against the evil frats this morning. As Patrice smears white paint on my face, I'm reminded of when my mother first taught me how to wear makeup. I smile.

"Patrice, how does looking pale make me scary?"

"The white just makes the gray shadow and red blood stand out."

"Oh."

That's all I can manage as I look in the mirror. Ceresa has now applied some of the gray and red Patrice mentioned. It's a dramatic change, and I do feel scary. With the lighting, props, and costumes I hope I will be terrifying. After that, Tiff and I follow Matt and Ed's lead and begin organizing the racks by rooms. We hand-make cardboard dividers labeling each. The guys have moved all of the props, and Bill has helped them set up. It seems that everything is prepared. I wonder what we'll do for the rest of the time before the haunted house opens. As if on cue, Bill addresses the entire group.

"Good work, everybody. I'm very impressed with your organization. Thank you. Now begins the time for rehearsals. You don't want to be caught off guard when customers are here. You'll need to memorize the hidden doors and hallways so you can move without being seen. First, we'll rehearse each room one at a time. The ones who aren't involved will walk through as if they're the customers. Then, after each room is perfected, we'll have a rehearsal of the entire house. You'll have to watch your time as you move from room to room to be sure you'll beat the customers to your location."

The next hours we all work well together acting out each room. It's fun. Everyone is in high spirits, playing jokes on each other here and there. Josh barely talks to me. I'm ashamed. How did I let myself believe it could be a possibility? I did enjoy writing the lines of our room, and the other two rooms' teams see my talent and ask me to help them too. It's utterly exhilarating. I would be thoroughly pleased if there wasn't a slight twinge of suffering every time I look his way. Maybe no matter how great the guy, romance is hazardous for me. He appears to be watching me. Is he mocking me? I did enjoy when he drew the pictures of the rooms to complement my writing. His pictures are gifted, and they seem to capture details my words fail to. My thoughts are gravitating to him again. I have to change something.

So I go over to Matt and Ed and ask (I know this is a risk, but I'm going crazy), "Hey guys, can I help you with your room?" Perhaps I can find out more about their evil ways working with them; be prepared for their actions.

They answer immediately in unison. "Of course you can. Come on."

I follow them to their room but notice out of the corner of my eye not only Josh looking at us angrily, but also Tiff watching my moves in frustration. She even stands to head my direction a second too late. What's going on? Here I thought I was distancing myself from the drama. I should be safe from these guys in public. They wouldn't try anything crazy here, right? It's not like I'm siding with the arch nemesis. I'm just helping prepare their room of the haunted house. They're employees here too.

First, Matt and Ed begin acting their scene, costumes and all. I have to give them credit. They make such sudden movements, even I jump.

"Here, hold this skull above your head over there. We'd like to see if that place-ment works," Matt says.

"Yeah, just like that," Ed murmurs in my ear.

In my ear…how did he get here so quickly? I feel a spasm of panic. They're now circling me. Saying things I don't understand and then both are smiling. It feels as though I'm within a magic circle of salt, except instead of keeping evil out, I'm locked inside with demons.

Ed puts me over his shoulder and says, "See, I told you we could spook the best."

They carry me out of the room. To my relief, Ed sets me down.

Then Matt says something that has me pondering, "Better watch where you go. You tempt the demons."

I thank him and walk away. I'm not sure of what to make of that line. Are they targeting me? There seems to be more between Josh and them. Are they against me being with Josh? A sudden feeling of prehistoric self-preservation washes over me. My body wants to tense and hide, while my eyes jump about investigating my surroundings.

Tiff catches up to me and grabs my arm and asks, "Are you all right?"

"Of course I am, Tiff, they're just a couple of guys looking to scare someone yet again. We're in public so I don't think they could attack here. Guess the *Scream* masks aren't working as well as we had hoped."

Tiff drops her jaw. "So you don't know then, do you?"

"Know what, Tiff? Tell me. What else have you kept hidden from me?"

"They're closely aligned with the human trafficking in this area. How do you think their families came to so much money?" Tiff explains in a hushed whisper while she cups her mouth toward my ear. Here, my best friend has kept more from me when my perceptions of her used to be so strong. I guess her acting has hindered that ability for me. With the disruption of national law, some illegal activity has prospered. Human trafficking is hard to catch, jumping state lines by bribing guards.

I put my hands in my pockets to hide their shaking. I try sarcasm on Tiff even though I know she reads through it most of the time.

"Oh, but what does that have to do with me?" I ask. So much has gone on, I'm in a whirlwind of puzzle pieces that I can't fit together.

Tiff just puts her hand on my shoulder, shakes her head, and then walks away.

Well, I didn't see that one coming. I knew they were dangerous and giving Josh a concussion a few years back is inexcusable, but I still just believed them to be adventure-seeking. I didn't think they were intertwined with something so dangerous. Why am I struggling to engage my perceptions? Have there been too many new people introduced? Matt and Ed are characters that would fit in with our room of Exodus. Luckily, they leave. The tension that had permeated the room departs with them.

Everyone seems to be lighthearted as we rehearse the final room with Team Mummified. This is the team of people I'm not familiar with. They're full of laughter and seem to not carry the weight some of us do. Their room frightens us all.

Mummies pop out from everywhere, some of them just props and some the team themselves. They all seem very acrobatic and fall from places I wouldn't be able to reach or pop out of coffins with flips. It's a good closer.

We all go back to the inventory room and begin packing to leave. Luke and Tiff are talking about the room by Team Sinister. Luke acts out the corpse that chases people. He chases Tiff a couple steps and then grabs around her arms from behind. Their laughter brings a smile to my face. It's good to see Tiff happy. She's like the sister I never had. Ceresa makes a face at them, but Patrice nudges her with an elbow. Patrice makes a face at Ceresa, sticking her tongue out. Ceresa can't suppress her laughter. Ethan approaches us.

"Guys, want to drop by my mom's tonight and hang out?" He's bouncing on the balls of his feet as he eyes us all like a basketball player ready to start a game.

"You have a place?" The words leave my mouth before I consider what the statement sounds like.

"Yeah, surprise. My mom's an artist. She's rarely home, but when she is, it's not a place you want to be."

"I'm sorry; I just thought you didn't have a place."

"Don't worry about it. I know it's not the norm. My mom's been addicted for so long I don't even think I have a memory of her being sober. She beats on me quite a bit."

"She what? Ethan, you're a full-grown man. I mean I'm pretty sure you could beat most guys in a fight. You're tough."

"I know, but it's my mom and even though she's awful to me, I can't find it in me to fight back, so I just take it."

"That's terrible." I can't imagine what it would be like to have the only rock in your life abuse you.

"Na, she's not around like ninety-nine percent of the time. She won't be around tonight. She sold a piece of her artwork last week, so she's off to Vegas or something probably blowing all the money she made, but I know she paid the utility bills, so there's electricity and everything. Come on."

"We're in." Tiff accepts the invitation. Probably what I should've done right off rather than asking all these darned questions.

"Am I included?" Luke asks.

"Yeah, I know you're just stuck with Matt and Ed because of your fraternity. You never participate in their destruction. In fact, I feel a bit sorry for you, but if you tell them anything about this evening— especially where my mom's place is—I will beat you."

He jabs Luke in the arm and smiles.

"I promise. Not a word. I'll just tell them I went out to the bar and got so drunk I don't remember a thing about tonight."

"You Frats do that often?"

Ethan teases Luke, but I can tell it's companionable. Ceresa and Patrice put their backpacks on and look up.

"Let's go."

Tiff, Luke, and I grab our stuff and follow them out. Josh and Ethan are arguing about something, but I can't tell what it is. As we go outside, I wonder if we'll all fit in the vehicle. Ceresa has her little hatchback that she lives in some of the time so we can fit four people in that. I think it's green, but it's so old and weather worn I can't be sure. I see Luke has his black Ford Escape with tinted windows so looks like we'll be fine.

"I'll ride with Luke," Tiff says.

"Okay, Tiff. I'll ride with you," I say.

"I've got room for four," Ceresa says.

"We're in," Ethan and Patrice say together.

"Great, I get to ride with you lovebirds," Josh says as he walks toward the hatchback. Maybe he feels more comfortable with his buddies, but I wish he'd ride with us.

"No, we'll need you to give them directions if we lose them," Patrice says to Josh.

"Do we need to make any stops on the way, Ethan?" I ask before we leave, ignoring Josh's look of disappointment. Before Ethan is able to answer I have to change things up. "Hey, mind if I ride with you guys?" Hopefully, Tiff doesn't care.

"Nope. Hop in," Ethan answers and then continues our previous conversation. "We don't have to stop. Mom stocked the shelves when she got her check."

"Good. Hey, is something up with Josh? He doesn't seem to be himself."

"Oh, uh, you haven't heard, have you?" Patrice asks.

I can hear the sympathy in her words. Why is it that I still seem to be on the outside of everything? Why am I the last to know?

"No…what's going on?"

"Ed likes you. He warned Josh to keep his distance from you," Ethan says.

He seems to be sticking up for Josh. I wonder how long Matt and Ed have been trying to keep these guys under their thumbs.

"I wish those guys would just go away. Why does Ed have to bully? He doesn't have a chance with me even if Josh wasn't around."

"I think they just try to find the best ways to hurt us," Patrice says.

I don't know what to think about all this, but my heart hopes this is the only reason Josh has stayed away. I don't want him hurt, so I'll stay away too, but this fills my heart with pain.

We park on the street next to Ethan's house. It is huge. Well, huge by my standards. Since the largest place I've lived in is a three-bedroom ranch house, my standards are probably lower than the norm. There's an iron gate surrounding Ethan's house. It's dark, so it is difficult to make out much detail. Some lights are on. I jump when I see a silhouette in a window.

"I thought no one was home," I say to Ethan as I point to the window.

"My mom's an artist. It's just a manikin. Seems to keep burglars out of the house though," he answers with a smile.

"This place looks enormous," I say as we all pile out of the car.

"Well, Nelson-Atkins museum owns it. They allow my mom and me to live here as long as she continues to produce artwork that captures them."

"Wow, that's awesome."

We all walk up to the door. The glass door in front of it has decorative iron bars. The roof has three peaks and above the door there's an arch window. As we enter, there's a staircase leading to the second floor. That was the level where I saw the manikin. The room to the left is full of artwork and supplies. Another manikin gives me a start. A huge window allows the moonlight to shine in. The thought of working in such a beautiful room has desire coursing through my veins. The room to the right should be a dining room. A beautiful chandelier hangs from the ceiling, and the wall is covered with classic square trim. Rather than a dining table though there's a couch, some recliners, and a T.V. Connected to the T.V. is a game console with controllers. Josh and Ethan toss their backpacks down, sit on the couch, and turn on the game.

Josh looks at home. I wonder how often they stay here.

"I'll give you the grand tour. These two seem a bit occupied," Patrice says.

"I'll be in the kitchen," Ceresa says.

Luke, Tiff, and I follow Patrice and Ceresa as they walk us to the kitchen. A built-in cabinet looks like it should hold china plates. Instead of plates there are chips and granola bars and other food. I can tell this kitchen must have been built a while ago. It has metal shelves to make up for the lack of storage space. We move on to the final room on the first floor without Ceresa. It's the official living room. Shelves full of books surround the fireplace. I step toward the shelves and remove one of the books written by George R.R. Martin. It reminds me of the vintage Facebook post I'd seen by a teacher threatening her students that she'll ruin the T.V. series "Game of Thrones" surprise by telling them because she's read all the books. A smile tugs at my mouth.

Next, we go up the stairs. They're wood as all the floors have been throughout the house except for the tiled kitchen floor. The railings are traditional. As we come to the top, I see the manikin I spotted through the window. She's sitting on a trunk holding a magazine, appearing to be reading. Pretty realistic. There's a plant next to the trunk that I cannot name but can tell it's well maintained by how green it is. There are four more rooms up here. Patrice points down the hall.

"The room down there belongs to Ethan's mom. Do not enter that room."

Then she points to the room on the left at the top of the stairs.

"This is the guest room."

I see three different mattresses on the floor. Clothes are strewn precariously about the room. It appears multiple people live in this room. I only spot girls' clothes.

"Do you and Ceresa stay here?"

"Yeah, well unless I'm in Ethan's room." She blushes as she says this. "It's over here."

She points to the first room on the right of the stairs. I peek in and can see one bed and a dresser. This room is as messy as the other. Finally, she points to the last room.

"That's where Josh stays."

My heart rate speeds up just thinking of him. I see a mattress on the floor, piles of books, and art supplies. I want to see what kind of books he reads, and I can't hold myself back. I walk in and pick up a book. It's *Foundation* by Isaac Asimov. I wasn't able to follow that one as well as I would have liked. I pick up the next. It's one of the Dark

Tower books by Stephen King. I love this series. It looks like there's more Josh and I could talk about, *if* we were even talking.

Just then, as if on cue, he enters the room. I had not noticed that the others had left.

"I was just grabbing something quick," he says.

"Josh." I grip his hand.

"I, I can't, Austria," he says as his chin drops to his chest.

I touch his face and turn it up to me.

"Josh, I don't want you to get hurt, so I understand. I care about you. I wish there was something we could do."

"I'm used to my dreams being crushed. It's easier if you stay busy."

"Well, I'm not."

I peck kiss him lightly as I run my fingers through his hair. The electricity makes me lightheaded. I don't know how I've gone a second without this. I put my arms around his waist and lock my fingers so he can't run.

"Austria, this will just make it worse."

"I don't care. No one can see us, Josh. We can just keep it a secret."

"Not when you can't control the way you look at me."

"What way is that?"

"The way you're looking at me now."

He kisses me, more deeply than ever before. The heat between us burns yet feels remarkably good. He looks at me, and I can tell he cares, but then he looks away and hugs me. It feels like goodbye.

"Please," I say. I can feel my lower lip curling into a pout.

"No, Austria, I don't care what they do to me, but this will put you in danger, and I can't bear that."

He walks off. I can't slow my breathing enough to call after him. Part of me feels broken. I don't know what to do, so I just walk downstairs to see what everyone else is doing. Luke has joined Josh and Ethan playing video games. He seems to fit right in. I hear laughter from the formal living room and follow it. Ceresa, Patrice, and Tiff have set up a game of Euchre. I join as Tiff's partner. Ceresa and Patrice are pretty good. Tiff and I have to make some risky calls so we can get ahead. It's a close game, but we win in the end, even though I don't feel like a victor.

PROCURE

Ceresa jumps out of a pile of props, a jack in the box. The group of the acrobatic four, Team Mummified, that I don't really know, all pretend to be terrified. One puts the back of her hand against her forehead and pretends to faint. One guy puts his hand on his chest as though he's so panicked, he's having a heart attack. One girl runs a few steps away, swinging her arms over her head like an idiot. The last is holding his crotch looking embarrassed like he just soiled himself. I can't help but laugh. It feels good to laugh. I forget about my crazy Altered Helix. I forget about Josh and me not being able to have a relationship. I forget about the crazy shadows. I feel like one of them, having a good time. I feel like writing techniques and ideas can still be learned here.

I walk over to the group. They're possibly more people to interfere with my perceptions, but I joined the haunted house to broaden my horizons, so here we go.

"Ceresa, you crack me up. You're so energetic."

"Yeah, she's got spunk," says the girl who pretended to faint. She has kind eyes. Her face puckers when she smiles as if she just tasted a lemon.

"I'm Austria. You know Ceresa outside the haunted house?" I ask.

"Yeah. Hi, I'm Camille. Ceresa helped us get an apartment. All four of us live together. It's crowded, but we'd be on the streets I imagine by now, if it weren't for Ceresa."

I can see now that Ceresa's intimidating exterior is a cover. She found these four people a home when she doesn't have one of her own.

"And I'm Emmitt." The guy who faked the heart attack waves at me with a sly smile. He has dark skin. He has bright white teeth and when he smiles dimples show at the top of his cheeks near his eyes. I wave back at him.

"I'm Brittany," says a shy girl with curly dirty blonde hair. Her blue eyes stand out from the eyeliner that surrounds them. I can't believe this shy little thing was the one running with her arms swinging crazily over her head. I smile and nod my head.

"I'm Landon." This comes from the last one, a skinny guy with a criminal smile. He's the one who faked wetting his pants.

This group is feisty.

"You guys are lucky to have met Ceresa," I say as I nudge her and give her a nod of approval. She smiles back cautiously and then clears her throat as if to remain a person of leadership who doesn't joke around.

"I found them in the lobby of the Union Station after hours. They were lucky. Usually, just the first set of doors are left unlocked, but that night the guard forgot the final door that was closed after the last train," Ceresa says.

"That was a crazy night," Camille says. "We even camped out in the lobby of a hotel for a few hours before that. They kicked us out, so we had to move on."

"Yeah, whatever, you didn't get dehydrated because I was able to sneak into the closed bar and get you water," says Emmitt.

"I'm just glad we all had enough cash together to order a pizza that night," Landon says, rubbing his stomach.

"Yeah sure, we wouldn't have ended up in that mess if I hadn't refused to stay in the place we had. Thanks for having my back and sticking with me," Brittany says. She's running her finger up and down the outer seam of her jeans nervously. Her eyes keep darting around in fear. I wonder what happened that made her not want to stay in the place they had.

Ceresa puts her hand on Brittany's knee as if to say, "Do not feel guilty for that." It's as if she's silently reassuring Brittany that no one should ever disrespect her that way, and true friends would stick with her just like these guys did.

"I was more than happy to coax them into sharing an apartment. Since they were all okay sharing a place and I could put all their incomes together, it was no trouble at all."

Bill interrupts us. "Time for lunch. I don't have anything here today, so you'll all have to go out and scavenge for lunch on your own. Think you can handle that?"

I look over at Tiff and nod for her to join me with these kids. She and Luke head over to us. A stitch begins in my side at the sight of them. I wish so intensely that Josh and I could be together. But I need to keep my mind on the task at hand.

"Hey, Tiff. Know a good place for some grub?"

"You really have to ask, Austria?"

"Well, I was hoping to find something low-cost, high-flavor for my new friends here."

I introduce her to the four I just met. She appears to approve of Ceresa's kindness too.

"I think I have the perfect spot. Have you heard of the new joint, Zaina, near Twelfth and Main?"

"I've been looking forward to trying that place out," Luke says.

We all head out to Zaina. The prices are low, and the food is Mediterranean deliciousness. It's a "Bring Your Own Beer" joint that attracts a crowd. Luckily, it's within walking distance.

As we walk, I get to hear the stories of these new individuals I've been honored to meet.

"If you don't mind me asking, how did you guys end up living on the streets?" I ask the group.

Emmitt bursts in first. "We all have degrees, man. Graduated early from high school and had our degrees at age twenty. The recent economy caused us to be so underemployed that we didn't make enough to survive."

"We searched everywhere for jobs and found nothing," Camille adds.

"Do you know how disheartening it is to invest so much and not have the return expected?" Brittany asks. "Not only did we not receive graduate level jobs, we couldn't even find jobs that paid enough to cover living expenses. The ability to be independent was robbed from us," Brittany says. Now her shoulders aren't as slouched, and she seems more comfortable talking.

"We had all moved away from home. If we were to go back without a job and have to live with our parents, we'd all be seen as losers in our hometowns. Failures compared to the ones who had stayed and found jobs right out of high school," Landon says.

"That's awful, guys. I'm sorry," I say.

"Nah. It's a blessing in disguise. Instead of wasting years behind a desk, we've pulled together and are chasing our true dreams; anything can happen," Camille says.

"I'm really in the same spot as you guys. I have just decided to skip college to chase my dreams." I try to console them even though I can tell that's not what they want. I simply cannot resist the urge to comfort.

"You and Tiff should join us. We have enough room," Landon says, smiling. Brittany jabs him in the side.

"Well, what do you think I'm doing working at the haunted house with you?" I reply with a conspiratorial smile.

A rumble slowly stirs through the group. We look at each other and realize it's our stomachs. We walk a little faster to Zaina, laughing at each other's growling.

Zaina's packed. The line extends beyond the door. Maybe this wasn't the best choice.

"I might eat my arm if I have to wait much longer," Landon exclaims.

"Here, have some of my mints," Camille offers.

"You carry mints in your purse like my ma," Emmitt kids.

"Want to step outside and see if I fight like your ma too?"

Camille opens and shuts her hand together like a moving mouth and rolls her eyes. I notice Brittany roll her eyes at Landon as Camille does this. Then Brittany gives Emmitt a pointed look that silences whatever rebuke he was forming in his head.

The line has cleared, and we're inside. At least the service is fast, and the food's delicious. We order and find a few rare seats at the bar. We all gesture for Camille and Brittany to take the seats and, to my utter dismay, everyone insists that I take the third. I'd hoped that when I showed up to work the following day, people would realize my fainting was nothing. It appears I'll have to prove my ability. I do go ahead and take the seat as I want conversation to continue without a hitch like an argument over something so silly. So I'm sitting when conversation begins. Brittany grabs a newspaper placed on the ledge next to her that catches her attention.

"Did you hear about the disappearance?" Brittany inquires.

"What disappearance?" I ask.

"There was an athletic competition. I think most call it a triathlon, but I've never dared to compete in something like that. Everyone was biking, swimming and running, but part way through the run the competitors went through a wooded area and one of them didn't run out. When the competition was over, friends and family of the participant went looking, but came up empty handed. That was last week," Brittany explains.

"Whoa, I did not hear about that," I say as my mind reels. My father had been athletic and disappeared out of thin air. The experience of which Brittany speaks feels a little too close to home.

"Crazy," Ceresa says. "It happened in our sector too. I mean, yes, we have our 'every once in a while' runaway and disappearance, even death, on the streets, but this was different. This kid had come into the shelter looking clean-cut and well fed. He was athletic and looked like he'd outlast at least ninety percent of the folks we had in that night, but no one saw him again. He had confided in another young kid that he was on the run from people but couldn't specify who. That kid followed up with his family and friends to see if he had returned, but no one knew anything about his whereabouts."

"So any clue what it was? Could it have been drugs or a runaway?" Camille asks, full of questions.

"A couple of unidentified bodies have been located under bridges and in wooded areas of the city," Ceresa says. "They were cut open so bad. they'd bled all they could, and then someone had washed the blood away. It was as if they were gutted before they died. The forensics teams have seen nothing like this. They've recovered some blood cells but, so far, the results have been inconclusive. They say the DNA is like nothing they've seen before."

"Excuse me," Camille gets up and runs to the restroom. Brittany goes after her. Luke gives Ceresa a shake of the head as if disapproving of her going into such gory details. He puts an arm around Tiff. I look down at my hands. Sure enough, they're shaking. I'm grateful for the chair now. When Ceresa mentioned different DNA and being gutted in the same statement my breath stopped. I don't understand how they could be connected. It's not like the different DNA has much of an effect. The biggest perk seems to be the healing ability, but that didn't appear to be a bit of help to these people. Maybe their DNA wasn't the same as mine. I still feel a bit dizzy and probably as queasy as Camille did when she ran off to the restroom. Perfect timing, our food arrives.

I have to wait a few minutes for my stomach to settle, but I'm still hungry. I begin eating as soon as I think it's safe. The vegetarian platter is made of falafel with tahini and grape leaves. Even though my stomach is still upset, I chance a few bites. The food has a cleansing effect, but I'm still unable to manage more than the few bites. I wish it could erase the images that formed in my head.

Camille and Brittany have returned and are unable to even look at their gyro platters. It appears everybody was affected by the horrific conversation. No one's eating more than a small portion even though our stomachs still rumble. We finally decide we've had enough and head back to the haunted house. I'm relieved to be moving on. Thoughts keep entering my head. The only reason something's gutted is to get to the insides. Why had the bodies been gutted unless people were removing organs? Why would they do that? I look forward to returning to work. Funny that the thought of haunting should put me at ease and release my fears.

CREATION

The next day at the haunted house the shadows are back and in force. I feel as though they move with my pulse. I wonder if yesterday's conversation is causing me to imagine the shadows. As if reading my mind, one appears next to me. Nothing could be causing this shadow. No obstacles block the light there. The shadow seems to be in the shape of a person. Could it be my father? This shadow seems more aggressive than the others. I have to squeeze the pressure point between my thumb and forefinger in order to maintain my concentration. It's rehearsals again today. We're going through rooms one at a time. As we walk to the room by Team Decapitated, a shadow flows right in front of me. I reflexively take a step back and run into Jack.

"Sorry."

"No worries. Everything okay?"

"Yeah, I…just forgot something back in the inventory room. I'm going to go grab it. Can you let the others know if they look for me?"

"Sure thing, I understand."

I walk calmly as I pass the others, but as soon as I'm out of their sight I begin to jog. A shadow lifts from the floor and rises to the ceiling. Now I sprint to the inventory room. Why is the activity so high today? Do they feed off of my fear?

When I get to the room, I go directly to my bag and retrieve my water bottle. My mouth has gone dry from fear. I take a few gulps and feel a little better. I sit down. I have an odd sensation that is impossible to even put a word to. Something between intuition and déjà vu. My arms prickle with goosebumps. I turn to the mirror of the vanity I'm sitting at. I swear I see a shadow fly up to the ceiling in the corner. Now I have a feeling of recognition. I turn back to the mirror and my father is staring back right next to me.

This time he's not hazy. He looks as clear as if he were here for real. I'm afraid to turn to see if he's definitely there. What if he turns back to the hazy appearance or disappears when I do? Instead, I smile in the mirror at him.

"Remember that camping trip we took to the lake?"

Even his voice sounds real. I cannot suppress my smile. All of the anxiety I'd been feeling is gone.

"Yeah. I loved the S'mores we made, Father. No one else puts honey on their marshmallow."

"You loved your marshmallows slightly brown, and I liked mine burnt."

"I thought you were crazy when your marshmallow caught fire."

"Those were some good times. I liked teaching you to fish too."

"Father…I didn't catch a thing."

"It was still fun."

I want to turn and hug him so bad. Tears well up, but I push them back and swallow. I don't want my vision to go blurry while I can see him. I've always wondered what our relationship would be like now if he had lived.

"Austria."

"Yes?"

"Be careful." He's hunched forward as if telling me this in secret, and the tension in his shoulders causes me to feel a sense of urgency.

"You already--" I'm interrupted.

Jack and Lea come trotting into the room sweetly holding hands. I take my eyes away from my father for one second to see them in the mirror and when I look back at where my father had been, he's gone. I miss him already. The old feeling of loss is re-turning. I had been to counselors after he died. The pain never truly goes away, but life goes on. The pain's rearing its ugly head now. I stand to exit.

"Did you find what you forgot?" Jack asks.

"What? Oh, um… yeah. I just needed some water."

I grab my water bottle and bring it with me down the hall to rejoin the rehearsals. They help the hours pass. If I were alone, the pain would burn a bitter hole through me. After we're done, all I want to do is head home, make some hot cocoa—Father and I had that with the S'mores—and curl up in a soft blanket.

"Can I walk you home?"

He appears out of nowhere and is causing the tingling without even touching me now. I know who said those words from behind me.

"That would be excellent, Josh, but don't feel you HAVE to."

He puts his hands on my arms just above my elbows very gently and turns me to face him.

"Austria, I'm sorry for the distance these past few days. The feelings I have for you are so strong, they scare me," he says.

"Well, they scare me too, but we have to give it a shot, don't we? This is one of those once in a lifetime if you're lucky deals, right?" I answer.

His answering smile has me quivering. How does he pack such a punch in that smile? As we walk home, we talk about everything. He finally opens up to me without barriers. I don't know what caused this change, but I don't care. It causes the shield I've put up to begin to erode. I feel like I don't have to filter anything with him. He understands everything I say. Without the shields, a warmth like a blanket fresh out of the dryer wraps around me. I invite him in when we arrive. I'm finally getting time with him. And time it is. My skin tingles everywhere and I'm afraid it will be blotchy red for days. We discuss everything, memories, dreams, and plans. His presence takes away the pain I would've been feeling missing my father. By morning, we've decided our plans are going to intermingle, screw Matt and Ed. We kiss, and it feels like what I imagine a lightning bolt would feel like, shock and heat at an unimaginable rate. As he leaves, I'm already feeling the gaping hole I know his absence will cause.

AMOROUSNESS

The smell of coffee and bacon makes it hard to not run downstairs. Tiff must be cooking. Not only is she a talented actress, she's a fabulous cook too. I'm surprised I haven't gained ten pounds since becoming her roommate. I run out and grab our paper quickly. It's cold in my pajamas and slippers, bun on top of my head. The trees seem more colorful than usual. I guess fall has fully come around then. Leaves are luscious red, little chick yellow, and sunset orange. When I come back in, I can hear Tiff singing while she cooks. A smile spreads across my face. I try to sneak into the kitchen to surprise her, but she must have eyes in the back of her head.

"Spill it, Austria."

"What? I don't know what you're talking about."

She turns around with a spatula in her hand. Instead of a bun, her hair is held up with chopsticks. She's wearing a black apron with a picture of what looks like two chef's knives in the shape of an "X." The word "cuisine" encases them with ribbon. At first, she looks upset because I'm trying to withhold information from her. Then her face lights up with a smile as she rushes to me. She grabs my shoulders.

"Austria."

"What?"

"You're all lit up. Your cheeks are all rosy and your eyes are ablaze."

"Are you saying I don't always look like this?" I should know better. She knows I'm always sarcastic when I feel uncomfortable.

"Oh my goodness. Are you and Josh? Did you?"

"No, you know I'm waiting."

"But how, why do you look this way?"

"I think…we're…in…love."

"Eeek!"

She bounces as she screams and hugs me. She is very excited for me. Tiff's like my sister reading my every move. I begin to ponder. She'd already been happy and singing before she heard the news. It's not every day that I get breakfast from Chef Tiff. Her face seems to have a new glow to it this morning too.

"Tiff? Your turn, spill it."

As the last word leaves my mouth Luke walks into the kitchen. His hair stands on end. He smiles sheepishly with his perfectly sculpted lips. His puppy dog eyes look at me.

"Morning, Austria."

"Good morning, Luke."

He walks over to Tiff and pulls her into a hug. They're adorable. As he begins helping Tiff with breakfast, I become distraught. I should've invited Josh to breakfast. I should've cooked. Super healing DNA seems to have killed my domestic genes. I take my plate to the living room. I don't want to intrude on their time, and they can't keep their hands off each other anyway. At least Luke can drive us to the haunted house so that we don't have to walk.

##

Today we're going to scout the other haunted houses and make sure our ideas haven't been stolen. First, we all walk to the Edge of Hell. This is the biggest haunted house in the area. They are known as the masters of scare. We walk down the street as a group; I wonder what we look like to others. Three preppy frat guys, multiple restaurant employees, and four street kids. Oh, and Bill of course. He is bald and tall. He has a goofy, science teacher look. He wears clothes that fit in with the street kids: stained jeans and a dark T-shirt with a flannel shirt over it. His boots are black and probably have steel toes under the leather. His appearance is intimidating until he smiles. When he smiles you see him for the teddy bear he is. Someone who takes care of everybody.

The Edge of Hell does have one thing we don't. They have a slide five stories high. It's the ride from Heaven to Hell. I think our story lines and acting abilities have them beat though. The employees spot us.

"Think you'll last against competition like this, Bill?"

This must be the owner of the Edge of Hell. He's wearing a suit, and I think I've seen him somewhere before. His hair is slicked back. It finally registers; he's Adam Sheffield. He looks like the opposite of Bill. He gives the impression of being a professional and hard-working guy to hide the Satan he really is, who would help nobody, unless it benefitted him of course. Suddenly he and Bill exchange some sort of secret handshake. They seem like old buddies. I can't imagine Bill hanging out with this evil man. Bill speaks next.

"Hello, Adam. Hear about the new code they're trying to pass in order to help your movement? When are you going to leave us alone? We're not harming anyone. In fact, we're helping get people off the streets. We're helping stabilize welfare programs."

"Oh Bill, always such a chump. You know I have interest in these buildings now. I'm no magician, but we're going to do everything we can to gain control of the ones not generating a profit, including causing you some headaches. It's time to join my team and make more money doing this."

"I'm working on it. I have a few things up my sleeve. You know I can never join your team. I've been clean over ten years and I'm never going back."

"All right, well come in any time you want. Hope you got the sneak peek you were looking for. Maybe your little group of preschoolers can pick up a thing or two."

"Thanks, but I think we have things under control. You and your little monsters should come see our place sometime. Tell them to wear their Pull-Ups."

We all walk out. We're heading in a direction that's not the way to the other haunted houses. I thought we were going to look at multiple places, but it seems Bill has other ideas. I don't realize where he's leading us until we're in front of the Nelson-Atkins Art Museum, and I see the huge shuttlecock sculpture. What are we doing here?

"It came to my attention during our last visit that we have nothing to learn from the other houses. We're a unique haunted house. We do not spend tons of money trying to get the best scare tactic. We use our minds. We use art. Now I would like all of you to spend an hour in the museum and try to create something new."

I've always felt a breath of historical resonance upon entering such a place. The art museum is in an old building with cement columns and metal doors. The hard, solid stone of the outside juxtaposes the unexplainable beauty within. I can see why

Bill brought us here. Josh grabs my hand and pulls me to the Benton in Black and White exhibition. We pass by Matt and Ed on our way there. Matt looks at me and crosses his arms over his chest. Ed pops the knuckles in his hands, fisting them together while he leers at us. I swear if he were a dog, he'd be barking at us right now. Josh puts an arm around me and gives a defiant stare back as we walk by.

The first artwork we come to is called An American Treasure. It's in black and white like the rest of the pieces of this exhibit, but it sparks my interest. Clouds appear like fingers reaching to grab something. In between two of these fingers is a crescent moon that stands out even in the lack of color. I notice that it appears vitally close to the center. There's also a man facing away that, though his head's bent over so far one would fear he'll lose his cowboy hat, he appears to dominate the other people in the picture. He's also larger than the others as if closer to us. His arm hides in front of his belly. I get the feeling he could turn around any second and draw a gun on us. I shudder at the thought.

The next is of a woman at night. At least I assume that is the moon hidden behind those swirling clouds; it's hard to tell in black and white. She's at the edge of a field near the road sitting on a fence with a gas-powered lamp on the mailbox. She has in her hands a piece of paper like a letter from her love that she must read before taking one step away from the mailbox. I don't suppress my smile. She's barefoot and rests her foot on a rock. The two pieces contrast each other. One causes fear and the other joy. Emotions spurred from just lithographs. Josh smiles at me.

"You like Benton?"

"So far, yes."

"Good. Then you'll like the Reality and Fantasy: Land, Town and Sea exhibit."

His face lights up when I look at him with suspicion. How is he so sure I'll like it? Oh well, we have to cross to the other side of the museum, and he lets me loop my arm through his. The tingling this causes makes me wonder how I'm able to concentrate at all. I'm so interested to see if our tastes are the same or hear his opinion and thoughts on pieces that the tingle dulls. And then I'm lost again. As we enter the exhibit, I see what has to be at least a thousand different pieces. I'm drawn to a Giovanni Battista Piranesi black and white. There are tons of staircases and walkways that zigzag together. It makes me feel lost and found at the same time.

"This one makes me think of living in the alleys."

And now it gives me a whole new meaning. It's my turn to put my arm around Josh protectively. I gasp involuntarily. Josh looks at me and puts one of his arms around me so that we're in an embrace. His arms are strong. I can only imagine what they've endured.

"How did you sleep in a place like that? I'd be afraid to shut my eyes."

He smiles and lets out a snicker with an edge.

"I was too afraid to sleep in the beginning, but then I made friends on the streets in the area. We'd take turns keeping watch. We found enough things that could be used as weapons. If anyone unwanted approached, whoever was on watch would alert us all. Not many people want to take on an armed group. Some of the closest bonds I've made were formed in that alley."

"Wow. That's pretty cool that you had each other's backs like that."

"Yeah, definitely makes it a lot less lonely."

"I wonder if Tiff would take first watch for me if we were the ones in that alley."

I smile as I poke him in the ribs. He ducks and grabs my wrist playfully. I duck under his arm, causing him to spin. He loses his grip on my arm and I grab his.

"Looks like you'd do just fine and wouldn't need me to watch," Tiff states out of nowhere. I'd thought Josh and I were alone. I roll my eyes at her. I notice she's on Luke's arm.

"You should all just live in the basement of my parents' house. They'd never know," Luke offers.

"What would your friends think about that?" Ethan retorts.

How had I thought we were alone? My head must've been focused on the fantasy portion of the Reality and Fantasy: Land, Town and Sea exhibit.

"I'm sure your parents would love showing us all off to their clubs," Patrice adds.

"Oh, lay off, would you?" This comes from Lea. She and Jack are here too. She seemed quiet before, but now I see the rebel streak shining though.

"Want to join us one night if you're so tough?" Patrice baits Lea.

"I wouldn't have a problem with that. Jack?"

Jack has been silent. He's staring at the Giovanni Battista Piranesi black and white piece Josh and I had been looking at, chewing his fingernails.

"Too afraid?" Ethan asks the still mute Jack.

Jack clears his throat.

"How? How can you sleep in a place like that? Look at all the shadows the staircases cast."

Apparently, I'm not the only one afraid of shadows, but I'm sure it's for different reasons.

"Not much a little shadow can do to you," Patrice says.

I feel Josh's arms go around me. I'm shaking. I hadn't realized it until I felt his solid arms around mine. He looks me in the eyes, but I can't. I just can't confess to him about the shadows I see. He'll think I'm unbalanced.

"Deal. I'm in," Jack says.

"I say we all live on the streets tonight," Patrice says.

Tiff, Luke, and I shrug our shoulders as if this is no big deal.

Everyone looks at each other. It's most of the couples from the employees here. Lea and Jack, Patrice and Ethan, Tiff and Luke, Josh and I, and Ceresa. Well, this will make for an interesting night on the streets. I'm curious and excited by the idea. I begin to give my approval when I'm interrupted.

"Only one way I'll follow you all out there. We have to get something decent to eat first. Let's all go to The Cashew," Tiff says.

VAGABONDS

All four couples and Ceresa wait for a bus to take us from the Nelson to The Cashew. We're all discussing different things we saw at the gallery. Many pieces could inspire new rooms at our haunted house. The moon is full and lights the street with a bluish glow. There are a few figures at the bus stop with us, but not the shadows I fear. A couple of them begin a conversation with Ethan as we near. I wonder if they're street kids. The one who isn't making conversation, but sitting by himself, seems to be on edge. He keeps rocking back and forth. Now Jack begins an animated description of his favorite painting at the gallery. The moon acts as a spotlight as he releases his acting abilities.

At one point, he bends over near the man on edge. I see the man's eyes dart toward Jack and his hand reach for his pocket. Before I even have the chance to take a step forward or get a sound through my throat that now feels stuffed with wool, the man hits Jack on the head with a coffee mug. Then he runs off before anyone can react and chase him down. That's not the only reason no one runs after him. Three security-looking guys have materialized in front of us and keep us back from Jack too. These were the ones I'd assumed to be street kids that had been talking to Ethan. A woman's kneeling next to Jack. I recognize her. She's the nurse who drew my blood at Dr. Shipley's. *What in the world is she doing out here?* As if on cue one of the security-looking guys in front of us speaks.

"We're a medical team working pro bono on the streets in attempt to make it a safer place."

"What are you doing to him?" I ask.

The nurse answers without looking up. "I'm assessing his injury. He could have a concussion."

She has a small flashlight and is shining it in Jack's eyes. He's responding and seems to be okay. It feels as though she's violating my little brother. If it weren't for the barricade of security, I would go to him and shove her away.

"What happened? Why did I get hit in the head?"

"You seem to be fine. No concussion. You may return to your friends in a minute. I just need to run a test to be sure the attacker didn't infect you with anything."

"Am I bleeding? I don't see any blood. How could I be infected?"

"Sorry, protocol."

Then I see the nurse rub Jack's arm with an antiseptic wipe and poke him with a needle. By the time she's swirling the vial, I have to put my hands on my knees and take a deep breath in order to not pass out. Josh puts a reassuring hand on my back and gives me a sympathetic look. He looks up when Jack begins walking. Jack returns to the group with a Band-Aid on his arm and a bump on his head, but in good condition. I still feel violated. What's with that woman and blood? I picture her in my head with vampire fangs. If I ever return to the doctor, there's no way that woman is touching an inch of me.

"What the hell was that?" I say to everyone.

"What happened?" Jack asks, still mystified by the entire happening.

"The crazy man on the bench hit you upside the head with a coffee mug. You must have a hard head to not have any cuts," Patrice answers.

"What did I do to him?"

"Nothing. He was just out of it, kid," Josh says as he gives Jack a reassuring pat on the shoulder. But I get the feeling that this was somehow all staged. Just like with the explosion, my visions seem to be blocked.

"At least the needle that lady used didn't feel as bad as when I donated blood for extra money."

The bus pulls up.

"So are you all still game? We happened to experience a mugging even before dinner," Ethan says.

"Nah, I'm in. Can't get any worse, can it?" Jack responds, full of energy.

"I wouldn't be so sure of that." Patrice places her hands on her hips as she talks to Jack.

We all pile onto the bus. Luke gets on first and pays everyone's fare.

"Not really going to be like experiencing living on the street if you're able to pay for everything," Ethan kids Luke.

"That begins after dinner," Luke answers with a smile and a nod.

"I can't wait to get to The Cashew," Tiff adds.

"Me either. I love their Fromage-a-trois," Lea says.

"Fromage-a-what? Sounds good to me," Ethan says with a sly smile and a nod of approval as Patrice punches him in the arm.

"Oh yes, Vive-la-cheese is what The Cashew claims. And Ethan, get your head out of the gutter," Tiff says.

My favorite dish there is the Black & Bleu, but my appetite seems to be evading me yet again. The bus ride isn't too long, but everyone else is so starved that they wolf their food down in less than ten minutes. All of a sudden, I find myself nervous about the prospect of living as street kids for a night, especially putting Jack in danger. I mean, it's the time of year that nights get cold around here. A shiver runs through me before we even exit.

"Austria, you didn't eat a thing. Are you sure you're up for this?" Josh asks me aside from the group. I can't let them go alone, so I speak to the group as a whole in answer.

"So what do we do first?" I ask, hoping to borrow some of their excitement and lose my inhibitions.

"Part of the beauty of living on the street is that there isn't really a schedule you have to adhere to," Patrice says.

"Let's take the bus to Broadway and Westport. We can hang out at Broadway Café for a bit. Some of our buddies should be there at this time of night," Ethan says.

We all load onto the bus, paying our own fares this time. I notice Josh, Ceresa, Ethan, and Patrice pay in all coins. I wonder if they panhandle during the day. It's a hard picture to form in my mind. Jack and Lea are bug-eyed and holding onto each other for dear life. The night has only begun, but, then again, Jack did just encounter something none of us had planned on. We make it to our destination, and I can hear the nightlife outside before we exit.

"Broadway Café backs up to Harpo's. A lot of businesses have happy hour there, and it only gets louder and livelier as the night continues," Josh informs me.

We hold hands as we enter the café. It feels like our hands were meant for one another since the beginning of time. I don't feel self-conscious holding hands with a street kid. I feel proud. It kind of surprises me. My mother would never approve of any of this. A couple girls wave and tell Josh hello. I feel jealous, wanting to claim him as mine. He squeezes my hand. How did he know to do that? We all walk up to a big table. There are newspapers and magazines. There's also a chess table; Josh and I chose to sit by it.

"How good are you at Chess?" he asks.

"Decent."

"Oh yeah?"

"Scared to find out?"

We begin our game while listening to the others.

"Did you hear Bill and that man talking about the codes? It sounds like the government's going to make it more difficult to house us," Patrice comments.

"We should start a petition. Hey, did you hear about the gal that had an apartment improvement contest for teens without homes? That was pretty cool. Is there anything else like that going on?" Tiff asks.

"Yeah. Actually, Ceresa's trying to start a place of her own. She and Josh understand what the foster system's like. The ratio of kids that actually find permanent homes compared to kids that don't is excruciatingly small. Once they're teenagers, fosters don't even want them. They turn to the streets. These apartments were able to house a quarter of them, but they were in horrible condition. The continued improvement contests have now made half of the apartments decent living quarters. Ceresa hopes to be able to house the remaining teens without homes. Not many are runaways from abusive homes like Ethan and me." Patrice explains as she looks into Ethan's eyes and hooks her arm into his.

"Yeah, but it's difficult to get started when the government requires so many documents to be filled out and taxes to be paid," Ceresa complains.

They seem so happy, after having been through so much. I look at Josh pondering the chess board. I really should've told him that I played this game nonstop growing up with my grandmother. I wonder what it was like for him to never be claimed. I still cannot fathom being without my father in my world. What is it like never to have that parent figure?

"You really shouldn't have moved your rook there," he says to me, looking up with his crystal blue eyes.

"Oh yeah, what are you going to do about it?"

"Take it." And he does.

"Shouldn't have done that," I say as I take his queen. My cheeks warm as his eyes become huge.

He sits and deliberates for a few moments.

"How's that Adam guy able to initiate bills for the buildings?" I ask to distract myself from staring at Josh.

"Adam wants to turn the Power & Light District into a complete attraction. Having those buildings could add hotels and restaurants to the area," Ethan answers.

"But don't the haunted houses attract customers to the area too?" I ask.

"Yeah, but not quite year-round yet like the other possibilities of the buildings could. We're trying to change that."

Josh moves a piece and smiles.

"Checkmate."

"What? Oh crap."

He leans across the table and kisses me. Warmth washes all over me like when you step into a hot shower. What was I thinking about again? Oh yeah. I have to move my jaw in a circle before I speak as my lips want to pucker back up. I really want to hear about what's going on with the codes. This is something that could affect Josh's life tremendously. I want to invite him to live with me, but I don't want it to appear like a handout to him. If he really knew how much it would benefit me, maybe he'd go for it. Maybe if I take a different approach, it will work.

"So when you guys didn't have a place to stay, did you ever build communities of your own without government involvement?" I dare to ask as this would be breaking the law.

"Well, come to think of it, I visited a location in the Northeast sector of the city that had dug underground caves and tunnels. Their hidden society went undetected for a couple of years. When the authorities found it, they kicked everyone out and bulldozed it all. I guess some of the inhabitants had been burglarizing local businesses. Had they not done that, the society probably would still be there today," Josh answers.

"Did you ever live there?" I ask.

"Yeah, but it wasn't for me. They were sort of hippies but enjoyed being separated from society. I thrive on society and couldn't stand more than a couple nights with them."

"All right, it's time to go." Ethan stands. I wasn't able to ask the question, but we have the entire night so there should be time.

We all stand and follow him into the night. He walks south on Broadway. Patrice is by his side. Tiff and Luke follow them first. Jack, Lea, and Ceresa are following next. Josh and I bring up the rear. When we reach 43rd Street, we turn left. There's a park that we all sit in. Like many parks in this city, there's a fountain in the center. This one isn't as big as some of the others. The angel in the center is a young child. It's sweet in the middle of this ghastly park; the bubbling water creates a peaceful meditation spot. The place makes me feel alone yet watched at the same time. A shiver runs up to my skull. My chin lurches forward in response.

"Who wants to check out The Levee?" Josh asks.

All of us but Ethan and Patrice raise our hands.

"You know we don't like to go to establishments that sell alcohol. Look at how abusive it turned our parents," Ethan says to Josh when he thinks no one else in the group can hear.

"I get it," Tiff says.

"I'll stay with them too," Luke volunteers.

I see Tiff's look of disappointment, but I don't want to leave Josh and since Jack appears to be interested, I feel committed to stay with them.

"There are ground apartments around the corner that are open to respectable looking street kids for restrooms, water, and a safe house if we need," Ethan says.

"Great." Tiff rolls her eyes.

"They're not that bad," Ceresa adds.

Jack, Lea, Josh, and I head up the hill to The Levee. I could hear the music from the park. As we walk closer, I recognize the band. It's Arctic Monkeys.

"What are they doing at The Levee?" I grab Josh's arm as I say this.

He smiles at the shock and excitement in my face.

"Sounds like they're starting 'Do I Wanna Know'"

I can't help myself. I begin jogging, my worries abandoning me in the thrill. The others join me. I can barely contain myself as we're carded at the door—luckily they allow ages seventeen and older. Once inside we head to the stage. I find myself falling into the rhythm of the crowd. The song seems fitting for our evening. Josh, Lea, and Jack surround me dancing. I look at them all with one of the biggest smiles I've had recently. I completely let go and let the music rule my body. I feel the beat pound through my chest. We're all shiny with sweat when we find a table upstairs after the song. Jack gets waters at the bar for us all. Now I find Josh putting a protective arm around my shoulders. I follow his eyes to see what he's looking at and find a group of guys that seem to be checking me and Lea out. I guess he's getting the jealous feeling that I had at the coffee shop.

Once our waters are guzzled down, an employee from The Levee approaches us and asks if we'll be making any purchases this evening. I notice Josh turn a shade red as the guys who had been looking at me now laugh behind their fists at us. We shake our heads no and head back out to meet up with the others. Another girl is with our friends. They're all talking about the stars and moon phases.

"Hey Tiff," I say.

"Hey yourself. How was it?"

"Guess who is performing…Arctic Monkeys."

"Get out. You suck even more now."

"Whatever."

"Oh, hey you all. This is Jenny," Tiff says to everybody, ignoring our bicker.

"She says she has an apartment and that we should stay with her tonight instead of under a bridge. I'm sure not going to stay under a bridge if she has an apartment," Luke says.

"What, you don't want the real feeling of being on the streets?" Ethan replies.

"There's a full moon out tonight, Ethan. You know how Gunner gets on full moons," Jenny points out.

"How'd you find an apartment?" Ethan asks.

"I got a job at the pizza joint connected to Kelly's Irish Pub."

"Sweet deal. So where's your place? I guess these yuppies can't handle the streets for real."

"We're going to have to walk halfway to the KCPT tower."

"We can handle a walk," Lea says eagerly.

We all begin walking north on Main Street. I'm again struck with wonder. What will people think seeing us all walking down the street together? Most of the people we pass by seem to be three sheets to the wind, so they're probably not in a judging mood. As we pass a liquor store, a man recognizes Josh.

"Hi, kid. How are you? Who's the sweet thang on your arm?" the man says.

"Hello, Tom. You didn't just buy a bottle, did you?"

"What's it to you?"

"Tom, it isn't quite 10 p.m. You can still make it to a meeting. It's on our way. We can walk you."

Tom doesn't say anything. He falls into step with us but stays a couple feet behind. This doesn't bother me as his odor is quite rancid. How many times has Josh saved this man from himself?

"It will be okay, Tom. Tom?"

We both turn around. He's gone. He disappeared without a sound. Well, I guess we won't be saving him tonight.

We get to the apartment. The building's another old, brick building. As we enter, I notice other people plan to stay here too.

"How many are you housing, Jenny?" Josh asks.

"I don't know. Ten to twenty depending on the night."

"Watch yourself. You're such a hard worker, and I would hate to see you taken advantage of."

"I can take care of myself. Thank you."

Whoa, I wonder if Josh and Jenny have a past. I find myself jealous without substantial evidence.

"Your group can stay in the living room. I have sleeping bags in the hallway closet. Due to the number of visitors, I'll need you to pair up and share the sleeping bags. I haven't paid all the utilities. It gets a little cold without heat, but you'll stay warm paired up. The water bill has been paid, so restrooms are available. Food is limited, but there's a convenience store down the block."

"Thanks, Jenny," Josh says.

"Not a problem."

My shoulders tense at their exchange, but I'm quickly relieved when I find Josh and myself sharing a sleeping bag.

It does get pretty cold in the night, but I'm warm being curled up next to Josh. I regret when I have to leave the comfort of the sleeping bag to use the restroom. I take care of business and wash my hands. As I'm about to turn the doorknob to leave, it twists, and the door opens. There's a young man I don't recognize in the doorway. He gives me a look that makes me feel ill; it doesn't take a strong perceptionist to know what want lies behind his eyes. He steps forward, and I feel his breath on me. It reeks of booze. I step to the side to go around him, but he blocks me with his arm. He grabs my left arm fiercely and holds my chin up with his other hand. I use my right hand to remove the hand under my chin.

"Such a pretty little thing. Don't you want to hang out with me?"

I try to scream but nothing comes out. I just shake my head from side to side. I bring my right elbow down on his forearm, hoping to release the grip. He yelps and I'm released. I take a step to the door, and he grabs me from behind. His arms are around mine. They squeeze so hard. Then he readjusts and now he holds both my arms with just his left arm. He starts reaching down my shirt with his right hand. I scream, but he claps his hand around my mouth. At least it's out of my shirt. I don't know if anyone heard the scream. I'm shaking with fear. He's bigger than I am. I stomp on his foot and bite his hand at the same time. He groans as he limps a little forward. He must be drunk. I try to take a step to get out, but he stumbles, and we both fall down. He's lost his grip on me. I pull myself forward away from him. He tries to grab my ankle. I kick at his hand with my other foot, but he gets my ankle. He begins pulling me toward him. Oh no, this is the worst possible position. Lying down as he pulls me under-neath him.

Then there's someone else. They punch the guy in the face. My attacker's head falls to the floor. It was a good punch. I think he's out. The person who punched him turns around and offers me a hand. It's Josh. Josh shoves the guy off me with his foot.

I can't talk. I grab Josh's hand, and he helps me up. He hugs me protectively. I'm still shaking. I can't make it stop. Tears well up in my eyes, but I don't want to cry. Josh seems to understand. He walks me to the closet and grabs a couple coats. We put them on, and he walks me outside.

"Austria, are you okay?"

"Yes," I say through chattering lips.

"I have to walk. Is that okay?"

We walk. My shaking subsides, but now I'm able to notice how much he's shaking.

"Are you okay?" I ask.

"Yeah, I just had to get out of there. The rage I felt was uncontrollable. What a jerk. I wanted to punch him again. Punch him over and over until no one would recognize his face."

"Josh, it's okay. We're out here. Try to calm down."

"Do you know what he would have done to you if I didn't get there in time?"

"Um, yeah, but do we really have to talk about it?"

The dark black sky is turning to a navy blue.

"Want to see one of the beauties of being a street kid?"

"I don't know how much more I can take, Josh. I guess I'm not built for living this way."

"This will be safe."

He holds my hand as we walk to the park on 31st Street. He takes me to a tree at the top of a hill. We climb it. He folds his hands and gives me a step up. We sit on a sturdy branch. He points to the east. The sky's now becoming lighter. There's a harmonious mixture of blue, orange, and red. The sun peeks out above the horizon. It's breathtaking. I curl into Josh's lap. He strokes my hair.

"What do you think?"

"I think it's gorgeous."

"Not as gorgeous as you."

I look up at him. He kisses me with a deep passion. I twist to face him more. Heat courses through my body as we kiss, erasing the hurt and fear. I feel like we're the only two people in this world, and this sunrise is meant for just us. When we come up for air, his eyes are dilated almost completely. They quickly change in the light, and I can see the blue again. He smiles and gives me a peck kiss.

"Happiest morning ever," he says.

I smile and embrace him. I'm amazed by how his emotion has changed. Maybe that's something you pick up when looking for a home on a daily basis.

How am I experiencing such polar opposites of emotion in such a short time?

"We should probably get back, so the others don't worry."

"Oh, they'll be fine." I hold onto him tighter.

"Austria."

"Josh?"

He exhales and smiles.

"Okay."

He helps me get down, and we walk back to the apartment. I hear a ruckus before entering. People are all yelling at one another as we walk in.

"You can't just tie people up in my apartment," Jenny's yelling at Patrice.

"He deserved it," Patrice answers.

Then I see what they're talking about. Patrice has my attacker duct-taped to a support beam. I can't hold back my smile. People have used markers to write on the duct tape that holds him up. All vile words and pictures. He's still unconscious. Probably passed out drunk. Patrice notices me and Josh. She looks at me.

"I saw what he did to you, but you and Josh disappeared before I could talk to you. I taped him up so he couldn't try anything like that on anyone else."

"Yes, but I don't want him stuck in my apartment." Jenny pouts.

Ethan takes out a pocketknife and begins cutting the tape. Josh holds the guy up so he won't fall and wake up. Just then, Jack strolls in with a shopping cart. They get the guy free and put him in the cart. Jack, Josh, and Ethan take him outside. I watch from the doorway.

"We should just push him down the hill on Main Street and let him roll," Jack kids.

"If I could be certain it wouldn't hurt an innocent bystander, I'd be all for that," Josh answers. I can see he's struggling to keep his smile hidden.

Instead, they push him to the convenience store parking lot. They return, and we all take a bus to the haunted house. On our way, we pass by a blood donation center. In our epiphany of what a life on the streets is like, we all decide to donate blood. When the needle enters my skin, I have to suppress the angst that rises within. I automatically look for the vampire nurse who had taken Jack's and my blood before. Afterward, Tiff and I walk home. Luke and Josh escort us. It's comforting having them there. We all take showers. I attempt to cook everyone breakfast. Everyone's polite as they slather jelly on my burnt toast and mix their scary looking eggs with sausage to make them taste better. They must not mind too much though, because all of the food is gone in five minutes. I smile. Maybe I can figure out this whole domestic thing.

SOLITARY

The days seem to breeze by with Josh. I'm walking on the clouds. We struggle to keep our hands to ourselves. Our spirits are only dampened when Bill receives a notice that Josh, Ceresa, and Patrice can no longer use the haunted house as a mailing address. Often street kids use shelters as an address on job applications. I think about Ethan's house, but he informs me that his mom would be kicked out by the Nelson Art Gallery if they house others officially. Bill has a meeting with the city and is able to work out a temporary deal. They won't have to worry for another six months about the address usage.

I don't even realize the time has passed when suddenly it's the night of the opening. We're all in full costume, including the hideous makeup. We're excited to finally put our practice into action on real customers. The first group that comes to the house is a bunch of high schoolers. They scream, and the girls cling to their guys. In fact, the first four groups appear to be teenagers, while this is entertaining, I'm growing bored and want a new genre of victims. Wow, this haunted house gig is positively getting to my thought processes. Ah, wonderful, the next group's a bunch of men who look pretty tough. Their muscles stretch their shirts. They have facial hair and tattoos. One even has a snake tattoo that slithers behind his ear and around his bald head. It almost appears to be a halo in the dark, but the head of the snake stretches over his forehead and the mouth is open above his eye as if to eat it. Spooking them will be quite a thrill. In the room, I helped to develop I stand still as a statue in my favorite vampire costume. I stay that way until they're inches away from me and then jump. They'd all been so transfixed on me that I truly frighten each and every one of them. This was pleasing. As I try to sneak to the hidden passageway that connects the rooms for us employees to move through without being seen by customers, I realize the men still have their gaze on me. I'm afraid to let the secret out, so I freeze. That's when I see Josh on the other side of the room, and I can't help but smile.

One second, I'm smiling at Josh full of love; the next scrounging for air as the cloth covering my mouth and nose will allow none. Someone has grabbed me and is holding something over my mouth. I feel myself being pulled back into the hidden passageway and then upward, but how could that be? There's no known exit above the passageway that I was pulled into. I was unable to make out any features of the man who took me, and I only assume it to be a man because of the sheer size of the hands, but now I'm blacking out. My last glimpse is of the roof, and I definitely feel the chill of the outside air before things go completely black. Great, I have no clue where I'm headed and then I awake just to more blackness. I try to feel around the room they seem to have put me in to make sense of anything at all. I'm alone in the dark but seem to be surrounded by walls. My eyes are slowly adjusting as there's a sliver of light coming from under what I assume to be a door. A door. Oh sweet escape. I crawl quietly to it as I press an ear to see if I can hear anything.

"Doc called in the information and sent a photograph."

"I don't know. Are you sure? Is it really her?"

"Yes, go see."

I don't react fast enough and "whack" the door smacks my head, lights out again.

The next hours pass slowly for me, and I'm unsure how long I was out or where I am or whose voices I hear on the other side of the door. I search the room for an escape and find only the door with the voices behind it. I heard them say "it is her"—they apparently believe I'm someone of value. They mentioned someone called Doc phoning information in. I remember Dr. Shipley's phone call after my appointment and him covering his mouth when I spotted him. They've more information about me than I realize. Someone's been clueing them in on my day-to-day tasks; feelings of betrayal twist inside. I wonder who it could be until they say names. Apparently, Matt and Ed have been filling them in. Of course they knew where I work, but what did Matt and Ed have to gain by the knowledge of who I am? I quickly remember something Tiff told me about Matt and Ed and human trafficking and fear rises within me. The voices outside the door mention that I'm his daughter. Could they actually be speaking of my father? How could they know or care who he was? He lived on the streets until he and my mother found an escape. They found a way to live a normal life, but how can this information be of such value to these men? Then they say things about my father I've never heard. By the physical description they give, I know it's him. No one else has a scar on the neck like he did or the star tattoo on his shoulder. Then they give me knowledge I've never known about him. They say he'd been an Olympic gold medalist before succumbing to the streets. How could this be? How have I never heard about this? I remember the sneakers and jersey I found in the box. Why had my mother never told me? Then I remember her being so worried after my doctor appointment. I never did find out what was bothering her. Why did I not ask her right then?

At that moment, the voices fade, and it becomes silent. This may be the only opportunity I have to escape. I quietly open the door and make a mental assessment of the room. I'm in a basement I believe by the cement walls, and I find the staircase that, hopefully, will lead to my freedom. I scan around to find the owners of the voices I'd heard. There are two men asleep on sofas with the television on low. One's the creepy snake tattoo guy. The sight of the gurney behind them and in front of the stairs puts my nerves on edge. What's that for? I don't even want to know. I tiptoe successfully by the two sleeping men and make it to the stairs. I have the first feeling of hope since this unfortunate adventure began while I'm climbing the stairs. This hope quickly fades as I open the door at the top of the steps to find another man, and this one's not asleep.

"Well, hello, Austria," he says with a sadistic smile.

I look around desperately for an out. I take the old-style phone on the counter next to me. This is one of the rotary dial phones you never see anymore, but I know it weighs a decent amount. As I lift it to hit the man on the side of the head, a hand grabs my wrist from behind. I know the face as I turn. It's Matt's face. How dare he do this? Then there's the sharp pain of a needle poking me in the arm. I don't know what they've just put in my system, but I instantly go limp. He catches me as I fall. The man I was going to smash with the phone grabs my legs. He and Matt carry me down the stairs to the gurney. They strap my arms and legs down at the wrists and ankles. I can't help thinking of the disappearances, special DNA, and gutted bodies. Now I see the other two men are awake and staring at me with smiles on their faces. I don't know if I black out this time from the drug or the inexplicable storm of psychotic images that flood my brain.

This is it. This is the end.

##

It's amazing how easy it is to let go when you realize you have no other choice. Something changes in my body. The blood flows so fiercely I must be bleeding out. I'm dizzy. There's a strong metallic scent. My eyes roll back. I must be spinning. Could every particle be floating away from me one by one? I feel weightless, as if I'm floating in the air. As if I don't have a body, but just my soul is rising. I feel emotions I've never felt. I don't have fear, anger, or regret. Facts and figures that I never knew before run through my head. I know planets that I've never seen in a textbook or on the internet. I know the rate at which a black hole rotates. I feel emotion from the clouds, empathetic with the wind. I feel love from the sun. Not just light and heat, but actual love like a dear friend's. What is all this?

I want to take a deep breath or smile, but neither of those physical things belong to me now. This means I have no physical pain either. I have no idea how long I've been gone. I get the feeling time here could pass very quickly. Although I'm not a parent, I get the strong sensation that this is what a parent feels like when their baby laughs for the first time. The thought reminds me of someone who enjoyed my first laugh. My mother. She'll be devastated. First, she loses my father and now me. It can't be. I have to get back. Then I feel the love of a sparkling star. It's like first love when you count down the seconds until you see the person again. Josh. This will break Josh's heart. He has no family. How do I get back? The desperate feeling I have is indescribable. How did I let myself go this far? It still is tempting, though. What am I talking about? I'm losing my mind. If I still have one left.

##

All of a sudden there's a forceful rush against me from all directions. Now my particles swirl at the same rate as a black hole. They're closing in on themselves. Forcing the small items to meld into a solid form. I hear sounds whirring past me. The light behind my closed lids is as bright as the sun but without the love. It's cold. I shiver. I shiver—that means my body's back. The metallic scent fades. My lungs expand with air. I exhale and try to open my eyes. I blink a few times. There are specks. Maybe I am still with the stars. Beyond the specks is a rectangular sun. No. That's a man-made light. I look down a bit. I see a board with names written on it, a T.V. and a generic picture of a flower in a nice frame. I'm lying down. Oh no. No. No. It's a gurney. Wait, I'm not strapped in. I look to my left. Josh sits asleep in a chair. Oh, Josh. I want to go to him, but I have tubes poking in my arm, and I'm not fully confident in this body being real yet. I watch him as he sleeps peacefully. I don't know if this is real or not. I try to soak in every detail. How long his eyelashes are and how he makes faces with his dreams. Then his breathing alters. He twitches. He's waking up.

EXTRICATED

When Josh wakes up this is what he tells me, reliving the memory:

I was lost in a misery I didn't know could exist within me, and if there's one thing I'm well acquainted with, it's misery. This misery was not like the freezing of my body in the streets in the dead of winter. This misery was the freezing of my soul. One second I saw you there by the hidden door the employees use to exit one haunting scene to the next unobserved. Your beauty had stunned me even covered with that decrepit vampire costume. The next second I saw a masked man with a cloth over your mouth. I didn't get to you before he took you through the door to the hallway. Some idiot, big men had been blocking my way. When I opened the door and walked into the hallway myself, I couldn't find you. I couldn't find you in any room of the haunted house, in any hidden passageway or even in the meeting room. Where could you be? You were missing. Now the misery I felt was much stronger than my soul being taken. This misery was worse than the lonely feeling of nothingness. The pain was unbearable. It made it difficult to think, but I needed to think clearly. I had to find you. I let the adrenaline take over as my search into the night began.

The worry I saw in Tiff's eyes was blinding. I noticed that Matt and Ed were nowhere to be seen either, and that was when I pulled Tiff aside. I had noticed her eyeing them skeptically before and assumed she knew something about them she did not trust either.

I said, "Tiff, have you seen Matt and/or Ed tonight?"

Tiff turned her face to me slowly and then, as if I'd unveiled something vital, her jaw dropped. I could see she was upset she hadn't noticed this before, but I didn't want guilt, just knowledge that could possibly help.

"I didn't notice that. I think that means they're involved in this. I know they're involved in an evil out there that I would never want Austria near. I'm sorry I ever brought her into this," Tiff had exclaimed.

"Don't blame yourself, Tiff. Let's just work together to bring her back," I answered. "What exactly is this evil they're involved in?" I asked her.

"Human trafficking."

"What? Damn it. Do you have any more information than that?"

We worked together to figure out how to get you back. She knew Matt and Ed were involved in a human trafficking ring nearby. She had even tailed them to see where they met. We decided to go to the nearest house immediately. We recruited the few we knew could help: Ethan, Ceresa, Patrice, and, believe it or not, Luke.

Apparently, living on the streets gave us some benefits as we knew our way around, could survive on little to nothing, and knew many kind and giving civilians in all areas. When we came closer to where the house Tiff had tailed them to was, we recognized the place. Then we put two and two together and realized what was happening there. The citizens who had come to this place had been citizens who regularly break the laws and reap power. They had also been seen leaving in hospital garments appearing to be recovering from something. An organ transplant, that's it.

"You're right, Tiff." I regretfully accepted your possible fate.

I wanted to storm in, beat the living shit out of everyone inside, and get you out. I had heard through the black market that this had been happening. Not human trafficking for slavery and/or prostitution. Those were scary enough, but they wanted you for healthy organs. This unnerved me. I revealed this knowledge to the others, and we began our advance into this house. It was like when we were planning out the haunted house. We thought about the entrances to the house we were aware of. We knew our cues and placement. Ceresa and Ethan, our best fighters, would distract the kidnappers while the rest of us got to you. We knew what roles we were to take. What we did not know was the setting of this scene. We did not know how many "customers" would be in attendance.

Patrice had a brilliant idea. She mentioned Gunner from the market. Gunner's a veteran who hasn't come into full grasp of reality since his return to civilian society. He is a good soul and doesn't intend harm, but every once in a while he thinks we're all enemies. I have never been to war, and I feel bad for him, but I sincerely hoped his wits were about him now. We were going to see if we could acquire sleeping gas and masks from him. When we reached him, he seemed together, and that was good. What he had for us was something he called ether. Given the urgency of the situation, we wasted no time with explanations and rushed back to the scene. We began searching out entryways for the ether. Luckily, although the air was frigid, almost every window was cracked. This had me second guessing. Wouldn't you be screaming if they were already in action with their plan? If not, did they already have you unconscious and if so, how much ether could your body handle? There wasn't enough time to play this fully out. We would just have to get you out as fast as we could.

The gas streamed into the house without a hitch. We'd covered our mouths and noses with masks to keep from passing out ourselves. As the thuds of bodies hitting the floor reached our ears, we made our entrance. This is when having Luke around was really helpful. While he didn't speak up in the beginning, he had now mustered the courage to tell us everything about this place. He told us you'd be in the basement and pointed to the door I assumed would be our entryway. I could see two of the men unconscious on the floor as I reached the top of the stairs. We made our way down. Now the true showstopper hit me. You lay there on the gurney, breathing tube in place and a fresh incision on your belly. What were we going to do? Did they make more headway than what I could see? There didn't seem to be any removed organs. The sight of the cooler in the corner of the room made me lose my balance, and I fell. I pulled myself up to the cooler to lift the lid. Nothing was inside. One positive after so many negatives! Now I thought aloud as I went to you and held your hand.

"How are we going to get her out of here? We need to keep oxygen on while she's out and, if we lift her, she may bleed to death."

Luke seemed to be more on our side than I would've ever imagined.

He said, "You know I'm in medical school, right?"

He began grabbing things and putting them to work. He assessed your wound and pronounced it to be only external damage. He started to stitch you up. Then he injected your body with two solutions. I hoped one was to wake you so you could breathe on your own, and then I prayed the second was something for the pain. He also removed the breathing tube, and I removed the restraints they had on you. Just then, one of the unconscious men began to stir. Ethan unleashed a violence I knew he worked his best to keep in check and knocked the man out in one swift move. We began our exit up the stairs. I heard another man mumbling something and Ceresa revealed the defensive tactics she picked up on the street. After one powerful kick to the man's jaw, he was sailing down the stairs. This ruckus woke the others so we began to run as fast as we could outside. I had no idea what we would do once we were out there, but the feeling of freedom was too strong to slow down.

The lights of cop cars as we exited assured me everything would be all right even though usually those cherries have me running, like when I was living in an old abandoned warehouse the state decided they did not want street kids inhabiting. I saw Bill at the front of the group holding his hands out to help all of us.

"How did you get here? How did you know? Oh, thank you, Bill," I breathed out.

"I went to check the market when you, Ethan, Ceresa, and Patrice all ran off. Gunner led me right to you and, lucky for you, was aware enough to be able to tell me what was going on. He didn't have the look in his eyes like when he sees everyone as enemies, so I knew it was true. What were you thinking, attempting this on your own?" Bill asked.

"We had to get to her in time, Bill. If we had been a minute later...." I could not bear to put the thought into words.

You were safe then and waking. You looked at me with desperate eyes and then looked around.

"You saved me," you said with a scratchy voice before you passed back out.

I stayed by your side as the ambulance took you to the nearest hospital. I felt a rush of relief as I saw the men being handcuffed and put in the back of police cruisers. You still weren't responding, but the paramedics said your vitals were stable. I was worried that you must be in shock and wanted to bring you out of it. I settled for just holding your hand. As they rolled you into the hospital, the doctors applauded Luke's work. Your incision appeared to be stitched as well as if one of them had held wielded the needle. Your vitals showed that he had effectively brought you out of the sleep those monsters had put you in. So why were you not waking? They told me you were in a state of shock, and we should allow you to rest. I stayed in your room and slept the

*rest of the night. When this morning came,
I saw you had risen before me.*

"*You should have woken me up, Austria.*"

I just smile at him. I can't believe he did
all of that for me. I'm so glad they came for
me. I'm so glad I still have my organs. I
touch my stomach and feel the stitches.
There's a little pain, but not much. I wonder
if the time I had been in shock was when I
was having the weird "out of body" experience. Then my mother walks in. She wears
a look of pain and regret, but not one of surprise as I expected.

"Mother, I'm fine," I say.

She half-runs to my side and embraces
me. I notice Josh looking at us with a long-
ing in his eyes. This must have been the
way he dreamed of his mother embracing
him.

"I'm safe. Josh saved me."

My mother looks at Josh and says thank
you with her eyes. She doesn't have to say
the words, and before Josh can even form

any in return, she has a bear hug on him. I can tell what he's thinking—so this is what kindness and warmth from a mother feels like. It has been too many years since he has felt this and I can tell he doesn't want to let go, but she releases him to turn her attention to me. I begin telling them what I remember, and I can tell Josh is calmed by the detail my mind is capable of recalling. I can tell he's also afraid, as he is unsure of how these memories are going to affect me. He has too many memories he wishes his mind would omit. Maybe it would have been better for me if I didn't remember any of it, is what they both seem to be thinking. The next statement from me has Josh wondering just as it had me.

"They said Father was an Olympian. Why had you never told me about that? Why did they know when I did not, and what does it mean?"

My mother is silent for only a heartbeat. The same fateful look of worry she had after the doctor visit has returned to her eyes.

"Oh darling, we had hoped you never would have to know this turmoil and felt it best for your safety for you not to know. Your father was a marvelous Olympian, and so was I, but that has all been stricken from the records. In the last events we participated in, they called us in for testing. Many of the Olympians had turned to steroids that year. But what bewildered your father and I is that while I was put in line with the rest, your father was pulled to another room with more official-looking doctors. What he told me, and this cannot go beyond this room..."

She hesitates to look at Josh and Bill, who had somehow appeared in the room without my notice. They both nod their willingness to comply with her request.

She continues, "They'd known something about your father before that day. Your father didn't take steroids, for he didn't require them. There was something in his DNA that made him stronger than the average human being. That day began our plight into the world of the streets and the unknown. We tried our best to make a living so that we could raise you out of harm's way, but the people who wanted your father's DNA wouldn't allow it. He ran off so that you and I could be free, and I've been able to hold my end of the bargain with him to keep your DNA a secret until this fall. I'm sorry I didn't tell you about this. He wanted you to have as normal a life as possible."

When she finishes, we're all struck silent. And then I regain my strength to speak.

"Thank you for telling me. It's not your fault. I wish I could've had more time with Father, but I understand his desire to keep me safe. He gave more to me than I'll ever be able to give in return. I'm glad you were able to keep us safe the past few years and, thanks to Josh, we're now safe again."

I rise from my bed. Maybe the DNA is stronger than I'd imagined. I give each of them a hug. We all look at each other and vow to keep the secret. If my DNA is different, like my father's DNA, are the people who captured me the same ones that were after my father?

INCOMPLETE

The doctors make me stay in the hospital for another day. I feel fine, but they want to monitor me. I'm afraid they will find more of what Dr. Shipley found. After a few tests turn out normal, I realize they must not be performing the same test he had. I guess he was specifically looking for the stronger DNA. He'd been right about the healing ability. The hospital staff is amazed by my fast recovery. It upsets me to be kept from the haunted house. Apparently, Bill has cashed in some debt from friends, and they're doing us all a favor working as security. It'll be safe for me to go back. I can't wait. After such a short time, I miss my new family. I wish I could make my sentence here speed up, but there's nothing to do. I read and write for a bit. After this, the exhaustion hits. Even if I do have special healing powers, I'm still tired by the trauma. I quickly doze off.

I fall into the dream easily. It's not a dream, but a nightmare. I'm back on the gurney strapped down. The same guys are around me, including Ed and Matt. They're talking.

"The shot you gave her will only keep her out for a few minutes. We need the anesthesia." This voice sounds like the man at the top of the stairs. The one I was going to hit with the phone. He's not just talking but giving orders. I think about Matt and Ed's involvement. Is it purely voluntary?

I hear movement and feel another poke but this time in my stomach. Then I feel a mask being placed over my mouth and nose.

"All right, this is your first time. You have to put a breathing tube like this in. Otherwise, she'll pass too soon for us to get the organs out in good enough condition for her type of DNA to survive."

Wait a minute. These guys do this for a living. Why are they training someone on me? Then I'm unable to form a thought. I feel searing pain. Something sharp is entering the skin in my abdomen. The pain sends tears into my closed eyes. I try to scream out, but my vocal cords are clogged with the breathing tube, and I'm unable to move any part of my body. The tube would probably muffle what little sound I could muster. Then the pulling begins. I'm in agony. This is a whole new pain mixed with the sensation between a burn and a broken bone. They're breaking open my skin. Why? Oh. I have special DNA with healing capabilities. Who knows how they could use my body? Since they're slicing my abdomen, I believe they must be after vital organs. I cannot breathe. I black out.

"It's okay. You are in the hospital now, Austria."

I open my eyes in my dream, but my dream has changed. I see my father now. He's clear and in front of me with his hand on my cheek. The warmth almost makes me forget every fear, but not completely. I try to imagine what he went through. What pain he may have endured.

"Father, it was awful."

"I know, honey. But not now. You're stitched and safe. You are safe."

"You keep saying 'you' very emphatically."

"I know, honey."

"So who is not safe?"

"It's still not safe for all, Austria. You're right. You'll also have to continue to keep yourself safe, too."

"What do you mean? They've arrested the perpetrators."

"You really think they're the only ones?" He's leaning nonchalantly on something outside of my vision's periphery.

"Well, uh, really, there's more?"

"Yes." Now it's as though he's taking an aggressive step forward to reach me.

"Wouldn't it be a little suicidal for them to come after me again? I mean, the police and community know it was me that was targeted."

"Oh, Austria, there's so much to explain."

"Well, you're here now. It's been so long. Why now? Do I have to be in danger for you to be able to converse with me?"

"Austria, there's too much going on to get into it now."

"Wait. Mother said you ran…Father, are you dead?"

"That's something for the scientists to debate."

"What?"

"I'm running out of time, honey. Listen. They're coming back. Just as I'm not the only one with my capabilities, you're not the only one with strong DNA."

"I'm so confused."

"Think. Did anyone else at the haunted house notice the shadows?"

"Not that I can think of."

"Did anyone else jump? Did anyone seem sensitive or keep extra quiet?"

I wake to a nurse taking my pulse. That was so odd. I hope I don't have recurring nightmares of being cut open. At least I saw Father. I haven't seen my father in so long, and now I see him all the time. It's never in the flesh though; only when I fainted, in the mirror, and my dreams. I notice he didn't answer my question. Is my father somehow still alive? I have to find him. He was so worried. He tried to warn me before. I should have listened. He didn't really give me anything concrete to go on. I try to recall in my memories if someone else saw the shadows besides me. Nothing. How can I help?

The nurse removes my I.V. and applies gauze to my arm. Someone enters with food. I hadn't realized how hungry I'd become. I wonder if the healing process depletes me, causing drowsiness and malnourishment. I don't even attempt to smell or look at the food. I just gobble it down like I haven't eaten in ages. My mother enters the room.

"Hey."

She has a sparkle in her brown eyes. Her lips aren't full, yet they're more than thin strips. The upper lip has a perfect heart shape, and the bottom lip is round. Her dimples show on her cheeks when she smiles. Her nose is a little long, but thin. She always says to be glad I have my father's nose. The light in her eyes shows how much she has held on her shoulders throughout these years and how relieved she must be to be finally opening up about it. I'm seventeen. It's time for me to take the burden. Can you ever really get a parent to stop worrying, though?

"How are you, darling?"

"Ready to get out of here."

"Take things slow. There's no reason to hurry."

But there is. Father warned me something else was coming.

"Don't fret."

"It is such a relief to no longer be hiding things from you. I knew it was for your own protection, but I still felt guilty."

"What else is there?"

"Shortly before your father left, he claimed to have met others like him."

"Did he tell you who they were?"

"Unfortunately, no. He felt the knowledge would only put us in more danger."

"Mother."

"Yeah?"

"Is Father really dead?"

"I've had to tell myself that so I wouldn't go crazy missing him, looking for him and hoping for his return. I didn't want you to go through that pain either, but I don't know for sure if he is dead or alive."

"Oh."

I still hold back the conversations I've been having with him. Here she's finally sharing information with me and, in return, I'm withholding from her. It's just that I can see the pain in her eyes that has been building all these years. What if Father has never talked to her like he has me? Wouldn't that depress her a little? He's been the only love she's had. My heart aches just thinking about her having to let him go. I clear my throat to keep back the tears.

"Oh darling. I'm so sorry. This has to be so much. Please try to relax. We'll get it all worked out."

"Thanks. I am feeling much better."

I let her stroke my hair while I rest. I close my eyes and bring my breathing to shallow breaths so she will believe I'm asleep. I am actually thinking back on the days at the haunted house, trying to relive the moments when shadows had been around. Attempting to recollect any differences from the other employees.

The nurse enters again.

"The doctor's signing your release now."

"Thank you," my mother tells her as she begins packing some things she'd brought for me.

I get up and hug my mother.

"Do you want to stay with me?"

"That would be nice, but I think it will be good to get back to my place."

"I'm sure Tiff has been worried. You two are like sisters."

"Yeah, and it will be nice to hear about what's been going on in my absence."

"Okay, I'll give you a ride there."

I give my mother another hug and tell her I love her. As I exit her car and walk to the apartment, I find myself looking all around to be sure there isn't someone waiting to attack. I open the door and can immediately smell the food Tiff has cooked: steak, potatoes, and pie. My mouth begins watering. I set down the bag. I hear footsteps; not just one set. Tiff, Luke, and Josh run down the hall to me. I'm so happy to see them tears threaten to spill down my cheeks. They give me a group hug.

"So glad to see you're okay, Austria." Luke speaks first.

"Welcome home, Austria," Tiff adds.

"Missed you every second," Josh says.

I remember the sparkling star that made me feel love when I was unconscious. Josh is my sparkling star. I hug him, and he helps me to the table.

"Thank you guys so much. The food smells amazing, Tiff. Is that pecan pie I smell?"

"Your favorite. Consider it a homecoming gift."

We all sit and eat. The food's wonderful. The steak is cooked to perfection, and I don't know if it's the chives or cream, but the potatoes are scrumptious. It seems surreal to feel so normal after being through everything we've been through in the past few days. Then I remember my father warning me that it's not entirely safe. Josh grabs my hand under the table. I hadn't noticed, but my leg's bouncing in a nervous tic.

We all say goodnight and head to bed. Exhaustion hits, but I'm so happy to not be alone. I feel protected in this home and with him. Josh carries my bag to my room. He keeps watching me as we're getting ready for bed. I don't know if he's expecting me to break down, but I can see he's ready if I do. I probably would, but I'm too tired. He wraps his arms around me as we fall asleep.

The dream comes suddenly as they always do. I've been having so many recently, they feel eerily similar to reality. I'm going to have to focus to keep everything straight. I dream of Jack jumping when the makeup brush fell, but now I notice in the dream that his jump occurs a millisecond before the brush makes a sound. HE saw the shadow too. Then I remember us bumping each other when I saw the shadows in the hallway. I had stopped out of fear. Why had he not seen me, but run straight into me? Because HE was looking at the shadows too. Even his fear as he looked at the Giovanni Battista Piranesi black and white piece. My father had also seen shadows while in the haunted house building. The image of Dr. Shipley's nurse swirling the vial of his blood, after he was hit with the coffee mug, quickly flashes to her swirling my own. HE has different DNA too and now they're going after him. Little Jack, so young, he's such a great actor. He is so helpful and full of joy. He's always ready for adventure. I know he's only a few months younger than me, but I feel protective of him. I always have. Like the little brother I never had. They're going to try to cut him open and take his organs.

"NO, not Jack too," I scream as I sit up in bed.

ACKNOWLEDGMENTS

The transformation this novella has been through would not have been possible without many people. There's no way I can name them all, but I'd like to give it a try. They know how hard I've worked and how many years I've dedicated to books. First, I would like to thank the readers. You breathe life into books and for that I will be ever thankful. Next, I would like to thank the professionals that helped me trudge through this thing called publishing: everyone at Hypothesis Productions, Ben Furnish, Carol Cartaino, Dr. Luthi, Michael Neff, Brendan Deneen, Randi Hacker, the Lawrence SCBWI Critique Group, Amy Brewer, Patty Carothers, and Rick Miles. Next, I would like to thank my friends who saw me through dark times and helped me celebrate the good times too: Shana Bartlett, James Young, Miranda Nichols, Amy Garton, Stacked Book Club, Sarah Smith, and Cathy Wissing. Finally, I would like to thank my family for putting up with me: Nate, Ethan, Jenna, Vic Hurlbert, Debra Scarborough, Cassandra Hurlbert, Victor Hurlbert, Vondell Neill, and Peggy Hurlbert. If I inadvertently left someone off the list please let me know so I can add them to the next book.

ABOUT THE AUTHOR

Stephanie Hansen's short story, Break Time, and poetry has been featured in Mind's Eye literary magazine. The Kansas Writers Association published her short story, Existing Forces, appointing her as a noted author. She has held a deep passion for writing since early childhood, but a brush with death caused her to allow it to grow. She's part of an SCBWI critique group in Lawrence, KS and two local book clubs. She attends many writers' conferences including the New York Pitch, Penned Con, New Letters, All Write Now, Show Me Writers Master Class, BEA, and Nebraska Writers Guild conference as well as Book Fairs and Comic-Cons. She's a member of the deaf and hard of hearing community. https://www.authorstephaniehansen.com/